For being friends since eighth grade,
From candy corn to
Whatever the future holds

Congrats Kimberly !!
I hope you enjoy
the book!
Ottilie Weber

1

Lauren

No one ever said the end of the world would be quick and painless. Actually, no one would have ever thought it would have only partially ended. All that was left behind would fight and struggle, one side trying to kill, the other side trying to stay alive. Good against evil would not be swayed regardless of destruction, starvation, and the need for survival.

This mess started just short of a year ago. Our neighborhood was having one of those very family-oriented, corny block parties as a celebration for Labor Day, which it has every year. I, being seventeen at the time, didn't like being at the celebration at all. First of all, the party wasn't exactly for my age group. The parents thought we were still into the little ponies and treasure hunt games. Secondly, most of the kids in my neighborhood were younger than I was, and the few who were my age were able to escape the festivity. Later I would wonder, was it worth staying at the gathering and living or escaping the party and possibly dying?

I was hanging around my little brother, Sean, during the party since my parents were with the other adults. They wanted someone to stay with him, so he was being supervised. They were able to go drink while I was here waiting in line for a smelly animal, whose long face looked even more excited than mine at being there. I loved my brother, but I just didn't want to be outside on the blocked-off road, with people racing around who weren't ashamed to show their enthusiasm.

At the time, my brother was six and fearless. Slightly on the hyper side and full of questions, he tested my patience at times. At the moment, he was holding my hand, jumping up and down and searching for his miniature friend, Paige, so they could go on at the same time. My brother had a girlfriend.

I was single. Okay, so I went on a few dates. I didn't need a full hand to count the guys, but I just never really had a full-out, real boyfriend. I've never had the genuine, strong emotions toward any of the guys I went out with. It was frustrating.

"Lauren, there she is! Paige, over here!" yelled Sean, letting go of my hand to wave his in the air while still hopping about. I was starting to blame those double-chocolate cupcakes for his energy.

I smiled, not sure whether to be embarrassed or to think his behavior was adorable. A little girl with dark red hair in long pigtails came running over to us. She was wearing a yellow shirt with a big kitty on the front. Paige was wearing yellow shorts, one of those little kid matching outfits you later yell at your parents for, wondering what they were thinking when they bought it. Yet, Paige and my brother were too cute together.

That's when the sky started to get darker. The past week, the sky was getting an odd glow of obscurity, not that I really noticed since I always kept my shades closed from laziness until my mom threw a fit. The sun still set at night, but always had that little morning glow to it. Almost like a storm was about to start, but no rain ever fell. At this point, the sky wasn't pretty to look at, possibly looking worse than it had previously. The atmosphere gave me the chills, to be honest.

"Sean, you want to go in and watch a movie with Paige? It looks like it is going to start raining. I'll make you guys a big bowl of popcorn," I said, letting my voice fill with excitement to try and draw them in.

I really hoped they wouldn't pull the "*I haven't gone on the pony yet*" card. The sky was giving me the creeps and I wanted to get out of there. I shifted from one foot to the other with my arms crossed over my chest. They looked at each other and whispered, their tiny hands cupped to each other's ears. Then they both glanced at me and agreed to see a movie. I sighed in relief as I took their hands so we could stroll back to my house. I had to tell my parents and Paige's parents so they wouldn't worry when they didn't see us outside.

We walked to the Jones's back yard where most of the parents were sitting on the porch at the tables they had brought. Their laughter could be heard clear as a bell from the front yard where the horses were. Finally, I saw my parents sitting on deck furniture, drinking some form of alcohol that appeared summery with fun, tropical colors. Someone said something funny that had the parents howling once more. I would have needed aspirin if I were with them the whole time.

"Mom, Sean and Paige want to go watch a movie at our house. They're getting bored." I added the lie knowing she wouldn't care about that little detail because she'd see right through it.

We were close, and she knew her two children very well, our likes and dislikes even our very small habits. A lie could be sensed from another floor in or out of the house by my mother.

"Honey, didn't you at least try to have fun?" my mom asked, pushing a stray piece of hair behind my ear before looking down at my brother.

I looked into my mother's bright jean-blue eyes. I've got the same ones while my brother has green eyes. Sean and I both had the same auburn hair my mother had. Mine was curly like my grandpa's, and it fell two inches below my shoulders.

"Lauren, how about you take Cole and Jill with you to watch the movie? They've been here playing cards the whole time. They're probably bored out of their minds."

"Okay, Mom, I'll take them."

It wasn't like it would affect me. They would be watching a little kid movie. I didn't care. I had no problem admitting I still liked Disney movies.

I turned around to see Cole (who was sixteen) and Jill (who was fifteen) playing war with a deck of cards, looking really bored and sitting at a circular, wooden picnic table on the deck. Mandy, on the other side of the table, sat with her head rested on her folded arms. At nine years old, Mandy was an only child, so she attached herself to the other neighbors. I walked over to them with Paige and Sean at my side. They were whining about how they wanted the movie now. The movie that I had to talk them into seeing was now taking too long to get started for their taste.

"You guys want to get out of here and watch a movie at our house?"

The two of them gazed at the cards as the parents continued with high pitched laughter and then glanced at each other. They got up and trailed the three of us to my house. The door was unlocked since my parents lived next door and the whole neighborhood was outside, so we didn't have to bother with carrying around keys. I pushed open the door; then the six of us headed downstairs to the basement. Flicking on the lights, we got to the corner of the basement, which my father had separated from the rest of the basement. In this spot my dad built a sound-proof room so everyone in the house wouldn't have to listen to the video games or the shows that would be playing.

We walked in and I closed the door behind us. Sean and Paige ran over to the shelves of movies in order to pick one they both would like. Their eyes gazed at each title. The other three went to the table and started a new game of cards, whispering to each other. I guess they couldn't really talk with the adults always chuckling. It was always a lot easier to talk when the adults weren't in hearing range. I was the same way at times.

The two finally picked some Disney movie so I set it up and then sat on the couch with them. I put my thin-rimmed glasses on so I could get the screen to focus a little better. Forty minutes into the movie, when all of us were settled and calm, it started. The house began to vibrate, and the TV went black. The lights flickered, then went completely off. The two little ones bellowed in annoyance, but that quickly turned into apprehension. My nerves were set off as I felt my hands start to shake along with the rest of the house.

Thinking quickly, I pushed all six of us under the table that just a moment ago was the home of a card game. I mentally thanked my mom for putting the old kitchen table down here instead of getting rid of it. I drew Sean closer to me as we squeezed as close as possible in order to fit. I buried my face in my brother's hair as I felt the fear of death breathing down my neck.

As the tremor continued, heat and a gagging smell filled the basement. Paige started to cry into my shoulder while holding tightly to me. Her tiny fingers gripped the top of my shirt. I wrapped an arm around Paige to bring her closer to Sean and me. I could feel the sweat on my body from the heat, but I didn't care. All that mattered was getting through this.

The sounds of wood buckling, and glass shattering were muted against the clashing noises that I couldn't pinpoint. The TV fell over and the screen shattered, shooting glass fragments around the room. The shelves that once held DVD's and games quivered before collapsing to the ground.

After what felt like forever, though it was more likely just over an hour, the earth started to wobble less. Eventually, it completely stopped, and the world seemed still. It took me a bit to even realize the shaking had stopped. The sudden quiet left a new air of heat on top of the New Jersey humidity, which already lingered over the state. A weird stench filled my nose, nearly burning the inside of my nostrils. I didn't want to move for fear the floor would be taken from right under me. My legs were probably as undependable as the house had been just a moment ago. Slowly, I let go of the two little ones to creep out from under the table. I had to pry their fingers from me. None of us wanted to let go.

"Where are you going?" asked Cole, looking very worried.

The others were appearing more frightened than him. All of them were still clinging to one another. Mandy was holding onto Jill, trembling. Jill's dark eyes were wide with fear as she held onto Cole. Paige and Sean attached themselves to Cole since I was gone. They were too petrified to move.

"Stay there, you guys. I'm going to see what just happened."

"I'll go with you," said Cole, starting to shift to see if he could find a way out from underneath the table.

"Cole, stay with them." I tried to muster up a hiss of an order, yet my voice wavered. "Someone needs to keep an eye on everyone, so you stay."

I tiptoed toward the door. Each step was hesitant. I was preparing for the floor to start moving again. I could see the door only because steam poured through the cracks of the frame. I went to open the door, but I could feel the heat radiating from the door knob a few inches above it. Knowing I had to go through, I grabbed the blanket from the couch and wrapped it around the knob so I would be able to turn it.

When it swung open, I never thought I would witness anything like it. In front of the door, a rock the size of half my house blocked the stairs, a searing smoke emanating from it. The little of the sky that could be seen was black, and an eerie red glow striped the dark clouds. Utter silence has never sat well with me. There wasn't even any laughter from where the parents were.

We needed to get out of there right now. This was all very, very bad. "Hello! Someone, help us!" I screamed, my voice cracking with panic several times.

After what seemed to be the hundredth time of high-pitched screeching for help, I felt tears in my eyes. Smoke drifted around me, irritating my throat and eyes. I fell to my knees, wondering what just happened and why no one was coming to help us. I coughed, feeling the smoke filling my lungs. My throat felt raw from the yelling. I knew I had to get the kids out of here if there was any chance of surviving. I got up and pushed some of the ash that was mixed with parts of my house off my legs. That was when I heard a sound.

"Help!" I screamed, feeling a little relief come.

I stared up in the haze to try to make out the face above me. I couldn't, but it was someone who could help us out of here. Ash, drywall, and God only knows what else was clogging my sight.

"Is someone down there?"

"Yes!" I shrieked, not able to hold back the jumpiness of my nerves. "Yes, there are six of us down here! Can you help us?"

"There are six of you?" His voice was deep. "So, more people did survive."

I took a deep breath because I felt sick after his last sentence. "What do you mean?" I questioned, not sure if he heard me.

"Hold on a second. I'll come down and help you guys!"

Rope appeared a few minutes later. I didn't bother moving, since I was stuck where I was. I watched the stranger as he lowered himself down to help us. When he was a few feet above the ground, he let go and landed right in front of me. By the little light provided by the scarlet, smoldering sky, I was just able to see who was standing in front of me. Part of the reason I could tell who it was is because I had seen him so often.

It was Aaron from school, who lived in the neighborhood behind my backyard. There was a good mile or mile and a half between our two neighborhoods. Aaron had fine blond hair that always had some thin strands falling into his razor-sharp, dark blue eyes. He was considered an unruly guy, who really didn't click with others outside his tiny group of friends. People from school couldn't tell if his circle was snotty or just didn't care to be around other people. Still, all the girls drooled over him and his friends. Seriously, some of the girls should carry a bucket around with them. As Aaron was looking at me, I noticed he had some residue smudged on his face and arms.

"Where are the others?" Aaron inquired and I was shocked he was talking to me; we really didn't talk in school.

I guess things had to change in our current situation.

"This way."

I trudged back through the rubble to where they were all still hiding under the table. They had listened to me, either from fear of me or the weather, I wasn't sure. I walked into the room and felt his five-foot nine body against my back, which was not shaking in alarm like mine. Sean must have seen me because he ran over to me and held on to my leg. Sean was followed by a just-as-spooked Paige. I had become like a sister to Paige from all the time the two of them spent together.

"The other people down here are children!" Aaron yelped.

I picked up Sean as Paige held my hand. I didn't care at the moment that Sean was getting too big for me to pick up. That was when Jill, Mandy, and Cole came out from beneath the table. Except now, Cole was standing tall, shoulders squared, his face blank. Was Cole trying to hide his horror?

"Lauren, have you seen what it looks like outside?" Aaron whispered into my ear.

"No, we were down here when the house started to shake. What happened?" I turned to look at him. Aaron's eyes met mine and I saw a seriousness that I had never thought that I would see in his eyes.

"You'll see soon. Now let's go."

He picked up Paige, who was still stunned from all of this. We moved collectively, staying close together through the steam and over the carnage of the room.

"Lauren, you stay down here and help the others down here go up the rope. I'll go up first and pull, okay? That way you'll have someone to help you up. I'll take the one of the younger ones on my back since they can't get up alone. Do you think you could carry one on your back as well as you climb?"

I looked into my brother's frightened green eyes. I felt like a failure and shook my head no. I was not even sure that I could get myself up, let alone with a six-year-old on my back.

"Lauren, give me your vest."

I stared confused as I handed over my vest. That was when I heard a ripping noise.

"Trust me. They need this more as a blindfold than you do for a fashion statement."

Aaron blindfolded Paige and Sean. My heart started to race with wonder of how bad it was up there that he needed to do this. Aaron handed Mandy one, but told her not to put it on until she climbed the rope. She nodded her head, still quivering.

Aaron put Paige on his back, and she held on for dear life to a guy she had never met before. He climbed the rope with ease. Mandy went up next, struggling with her chubby little-kid fingers while trying to stop shaking. I saw Aaron lean over the edge far and then pull her up.

Using her lean and toned sport-procured muscles, Jill climbed up. She wrapped her legs around the rope and drew herself up, making it look easier than Mandy had. Next, Cole ascended without saying a word, though he was having a harder time than Jill. Of course, I knew his pride wouldn't let him admit it. I had known these people all their lives. I'd seen them around and learned each of their quirks. I then realized Sean was still attached to me and I wasn't sure if

I would be able to scale the rope with him. I didn't have any upper body strength.

"Aaron, can you come down and bring Sean up with you?"

I held Sean unyieldingly, feeling that whatever was up there couldn't be good. Sean, with his blindfold on, gripped me tighter. He feared what he couldn't see, and I knew it. Aaron didn't answer, but I saw him coming down.

"Sean, listen to me. Aaron is going to carry you up the rope. I can't do it, but this is for your own good. I'm here to protect you. Always remember that," I whispered into his ear, hoping that my words were soothing him.

"Come on, Sean, you and I are going to climb the rope so you can be with your friends."

I could tell he was really trying to be comforting to Sean, possibly even to me, too.

"Is Paige there?" Sean asked in a timid voice.

"She's up there waiting for you," I replied in a low voice, thinking they were so innocent and lucky to have each other during something like this.

"Okay, you have to hold on really tightly."

Sean nodded as he held on. I watched Aaron, a guy that barely knew me, take my brother away. I took a deep breath, trying to calm my racing heart. I was going to be sick if I didn't calm down soon.

"Lauren, we're up and he's safe — it's your turn."

I wrapped my hands around the rope, hoping I could do this. I could almost hear the laughter from my old gym class in my ears as I pulled myself up. My muscles tightened as I kept pulling. The rope burned against my skin and I didn't think I could keep going. Aaron leaned over and pulled me up, just as he had done for Mandy. I finally had my feet on the ground and didn't even look at Aaron as I grabbed Sean close to me, closing my eyes against his head and held him.

"Thank you, Aaron," I murmured.

I bent down and held Paige, who had tears running down her face from under the blindfold, soaking the fabric. That was when I glanced up and I wished I hadn't. I turned to look at Aaron and he just nodded his head, unable to speak. My once manicured neighborhood seemed like another planet as a red glow enveloped it. A thick vapor rose high in the air, acting like a thick fog. Rocks the size of an average house were everywhere, mixed with the wreckage of what used to be where we lived. That was when I saw the reason for the blindfolds. Dead bodies littered the ground, destroyed to the point where I couldn't tell who used to be who. I thought I even saw bloodied hooves under a pile of debris. Behind me, Mandy started to throw up from the stench around us.

"I've been going around our area and I haven't found anyone except for you guys still alive." Aaron spoke in a low wounded voice in my ear so the others wouldn't hear.

I felt tears in my eyes, understanding that everyone from the party was now lying in their graves. Our friends, neighbors, and families were all dead. We only had each other. Aaron picked up Paige and was on the move over the ruins as the other two followed leading a blindfolded Mandy. I was in the back, holding Sean, his arms clenched around my neck. I tried to catch up with Aaron, hard to do as I was barefoot, and there were no soft surfaces to walk on. Rocks and who knows what stabbed the bottom of my feet. I nearly had to jump with each step, trying to hold back the whimpering that surfaced. Finally, I caught up so we could talk about what to do. I wasn't going to let us die now. We spoke in hushed tones so we wouldn't scare anyone.

"Aaron, what are we going to do?"

"We have to get away from the bodies, so we don't get sick from them or have to smell them." My eyes widened as he said that, and my jaw dropped. "Don't look at me like that! I know it's horrible, but it's true. I'll help you guys if you need the help with the kids."

"Thank you."

"I wasn't expecting to find kids or you down there." Aaron's voice sounded like he was somewhere else.

"I'm happy you found us. I thought we would be stuck down there until we…" I couldn't even say what I thought would have happened.

Aaron put an arm around my shoulders, bringing me close to him, rubbing my shoulder slightly. I looked at the ground, fearing to see the distorted bodies of everyone that I knew and grew up with. Aaron was steering me in an unknown direction. Cole and Jill were quiet behind us because they, like us, had seen what had happened. We walked to the pond, about a couple of miles from our homes. Then Aaron put Paige down to wash his face and hands in the water. There, on the opposite side of the lake, was a giant asteroid.

I placed Sean down, and then he and Paige took off their blindfolds. They sat by the water, putting their feet in it. I sat next to Aaron as he was cleaning himself off; dirty water dripped off his body. His sleeveless black shirt was covered in ash and plaster just like his jeans. I glanced down at my own red camisole and shorts. They weren't as dirty, but had some ash dusted on them.

"How did we not get warning of this?"

Aaron looked up, confused.

"Just about every country has a space program," I continued.

"They probably knew they couldn't do anything. Those aren't your average-size asteroids and they are supposed to shrink when they hit our atmosphere. So they knew that the end was here, so why send the world in an uproar when they knew it couldn't be stopped?"

I stared at the lake, seeing my own reflection in the water, the reddish haze of the air in the background. I drew my legs to my chest as a few silent tears fell down my face. My legs seemed to turn to jelly. Once I was down, there was no chance that I would be able to stand again. I really didn't care if anyone saw me. What does it matter now? We didn't even know who was still alive.

I glimpsed over at the other three who tried talking but weren't sure what to say. I saw Cole struggle to calm them down and I studied my reflection in the water. It appeared pathetic. Sean and Paige found a way to escape this if only for a moment. I wished I were in their shoes instead of my own right now. That was if I were wearing shoes.

"Hey, are you, all right?"

I glanced over at Aaron, who was titling his head at me. I felt stupid at the moment.

"Yeah, I'm fine. Can I ask you something?"

"Sure."

"Why are you helping us?"

"You have to be kidding me," Aaron started, pausing as he wiped his hands on his pants. "I'm not even going to answer such a stupid question. I'll say this though. You are a nice person, who puts up with a lot of crap from people at school, and you were in trouble. I was alone after watching my parents getting smashed by one of those rocks and I had to find someone who was alive. I walked around for an hour, trying to find someone who was at least moving, and I heard this little voice about to break out into tears. I had to save the person in tears."

"I'm so pathetic," I whispered as I buried my face into my knees.

"Self-pity later. Right now, we have to figure out how to stay alive and take care of them."

"At least someone has their head together," I half-muttered, half-sighed.

"Give yourself a few more minutes. We might also have some more trouble."

I let out a snort of laughter as I finally looked up at him. "You don't call this trouble?"

"Even more trouble."

"What? Are more rocks coming to kill us?" I asked dryly.

"No, Mr. Dean Manson is alive."

"Why does that name sound familiar?" I squinted, staring at him as I tried to search my files in my memory bank.

"He was the mayor here for years and was head of the police department at another point. I got him in trouble, which I'll explain later on, and he lost everything important in his life. He's been out to get me ever since. There isn't any order now, it seems, so this would be the prefect chance for him to get back at me."

"What could you have done for him to want to hurt you?" I asked, scrunching my eyebrows together.

He gave a weak smile and glanced at Sean and Paige playing in ankle-deep water.

"Let's not get into this now, okay?"

I nodded my head.

"Let's just leave it at it was really bad and he has been after my head since. Now, Dean Manson has the perfect chance to kill me."

I was going to be sick. I wrapped my arms around me tighter as I leaned my forehead on my knees. I wanted to be younger so I wouldn't have to be responsible. My stomach felt like it had been turned upside down.

"Look, I can see you're having a hard time with this—"

"Of course, I am. Everyone around here is dead and we don't know if it is like this at other places too. You just basically told me that the people that I grew up with are dead!" I spat.

"You have to be strong for your brother." Aaron barked.

That's when it hit me. I quickly turned to look at my brother. I had to take care of Sean. The reason Aaron was thinking clearly was because he knew that we had to focus to keep the children alive.

"So, the plan, I take it, is to look for those who are alive?" I inquired.

"Yeah, we have to see if it's like this in other areas... maybe even other states."

"It's going to be tough with little kids. They won't want to walk that far."

He smiled a small, sad smile. "I know, but if there are other people that can help us, it'll be better in the long run."

"Will you help us?" I questioned, hoping he would stay with us.

I really didn't know what I was doing, and to have another person to help I would be amazing.

"Yes, I'll do the best I can, but no promises. Just remember, Lauren, I can't always be with you guys since Manson is after me. I barely believed it myself when I saw him wandering around before I found you."

"I'll keep that in mind."

"We'll stay here tonight; then we move tomorrow."

"Sean, Paige, come here please," I called to them.

They ran, laughing happily, to Aaron and me. I hugged them close to me. They were soaking wet, and I was happy for the heat so they wouldn't get sick.

"Lauren, where is my mommy and daddy?" Paige spoke up.

My heart stopped.

"How about we go to sleep now, okay?" suggested Aaron, trying to get their minds off this.

"Awe, but I'm not tired," yawned Sean.

"Come on, you two. Lay here and go to sleep. Aaron and I need to talk for just a bit longer then I'll come, okay?"

They nodded, too worn out from the excitement of today. They fell asleep quickly. I got up and went after Aaron, who was with Jill, Cole, and Mandy. Mandy appeared to be in tears and Cole looked as if he was going to hit Aaron. So, I rushed over.

"What's going on?" I spoke in a low voice, hoping not to wake the little ones.

"Why should we listen to this guy?" Cole growled, his eyes still on Aaron. "Do we even know him?"

"I kind of know him from school, Cole... and he saved us!"

"Kind of? You're placing our lives in the hands of this jerk."

"Look here, kid," Aaron said, getting angry, and picked Cole up by his shirt collar. "I can go put you back there! Would you rather be with the bodies that got incinerated by the heat?"

"Stop! You two are making Mandy cry more!" Jill shouted as she bent down, wrapping her arms around Mandy.

"Guys, I get that we are all a little testy at the moment and I still don't have my wits on me, so please keep it together! Now go to sleep, so we can move tomorrow since we have to see if there are any areas around here that weren't affected by this."

Aaron dropped Cole onto the ground with a thud. Cole shot him a dirty look.

"Look, you three, Lauren and I are in charge. You can't go anywhere without either one of us. It's for your own good. If we have any chance of staying alive, you have to listen to us. Got it?"

Jill and Mandy nodded their heads and went to join Paige and Sean. Cole stood up and tried to stare down Aaron. My heart started racing, hoping Aaron wouldn't kill Cole now. Hadn't there been enough death today? I had seen the not-even-trying fights Aaron was in at school, and Cole wouldn't stand a chance. Cole has always been more talk then punch, even when we were little.

"I don't even know why Lauren is putting so much trust in you," Cole voiced roughly as he scowled at Aaron.

"Watch it, kid. Enough blood has been spilled today. Just go to bed before I kill you myself," Aaron muttered between gritted teeth.

Aaron gave Cole a small shove toward where we were all going to sleep; he stumbled only to turn and watch us, waiting for us to make our move. I walked over, leaving Aaron to follow me or stay there, giving him the choice on what to do. I sat by my brother's feet, not believing he could possibly be the only family I had left in the whole world. As two tears fell down my face, I pressed my hands over my eyes, trying to brush away the tears.

"Lauren, get some sleep. I'm a light sleeper so I'll make sure everything's all right," Aaron said softly.

I looked up at the guy who I barely talked

to at school. The guy whose table I couldn't even sit at because I wasn't on his or his friends' level of social being. I made a fool out of myself in front of him on numerous occasions in gym. Yet here he was. I slid down on the grass, knowing I wouldn't get any sleep, but I still tried. I brushed some of Sean's hair out of his face; he almost looked at peace. Through the whole hour of sleep, I managed to get that night, the dark horrors of what happened played before my eyes over and over.

2

Aaron

I watched Lauren fall asleep near her brother and his friends. I hated her at that moment. There really was no other way to express the feelings I had toward her. She had someone with her that she knew: family. Not only that, but a whole group of people while I didn't. I was alone. She had her brother — I had a man who wanted my head on his wall as a trophy. Looking at this strange cluster, I suddenly wondered why I was even helping them. Even, as this question seeped through my mind, it made me sick to my stomach. How could I look at them, especially the two kids, and doubt my decision?

I was never friends with Lauren. We'd had been on the same bus since kindergarten, until one of my buddies began to drive me to high school. She and I had a few classes together over the years, but Lauren was the silent one in the class, with the high stack of books, not daring to leave them in her locker because you might need one of the textbooks in class that day. She could be absolutely annoying. Was being a perfectionist really, honestly necessary? In my handbook of life—no.

After watching my parents being crushed as they tried to run for the house, I had to help when I heard her cry.

I saw it all happen as I was sitting on my windowsill with my window wide open, hanging a leg out while I was thinking. I was hot and needed some air. Mom didn't like when I sat like this, but I'd always found it relaxing. Then in the distance, there were bizarre shapes in the sky, and in a blink of an eye, scattered rocks the sizes of busses or bigger were heading toward the earth.

I closed my eyes quickly and shook my head to get the images out of my mind. I was not ready to face that. It was the first time a major feeling of guilt and horror took over me. The only family I had was killed before my eyes. They had put up with me, dealt with more than what they signed up for.

Listening closely to the air blow by, trying to make sure that no one was coming, I looked over at the six of them and I felt my heart race. Trying to calm down, I hung my head low to try and get my breathing back to normal. How did this whole mess happen? I just became an orphan for the second time in my life. The first time was miserable enough, but a second time? I just lost my all my friends. I was stuck with Lauren and her luggage. After what seemed like forever, one of the kids started to move, which made Lauren come around.

She sat up appearing like she hadn't really slept either. Her eyelids looked heavy with dark circles, not all of which seemed to be from her make-up. Lauren rubbed her head, then stretched her limbs a little. Her jean-blue eyes met with mine and they were filled with pain, as she remembered what happened. I noticed because it shined in her eyes and I was sure she could see the same shimmer in my own.

"We should go, so wake them up and we'll be out," I spoke softly.

She nodded and started to wake them up gently. I remembered when my mom did that for school or if I was sleeping in too late on the weekends and she thought I wouldn't be able to sleep that night. That would never happen again. She would tenderly rub my back until I made signs that I was alive. The two littlest ones started to stir, then got up, looking confused. Almost like they had forgotten that they fell asleep on the ground instead of their beds. That yesterday was nothing but a nightmare instead of reality.

Next, the other three woke up. We started moving, as the two little ones wondered where breakfast was. This was definitely going to be a long day, the first of many to come; I could feel it.

Lauren was walking in front with me as she held the two littlest ones by the hand. I could tell she wanted them to walk as far as they could because she wasn't going to be able to carry both of them for too long. Meanwhile, the three in the back were quiet, but Cole gave me death glares every once in a while. I could sense his glare on the back of my head, and I would turn my head as I felt the pricking. Our eyes would meet and we'd both scowl. I still couldn't figure out what I did to him.

"I want pancakes!" Sean pipped up, nearly skipping.

"Waffles!" Paige spoke, challenging Sean's food choice.

"Pancakes!"

"Waffles!"

"Guys, there aren't waffles *or* pancakes available right now," Lauren commented, sounding upset about them being hungry.

"But it's time for breakfast! I woke up, so it is time for food!"

I grinned, suppressing a chuckle. I really liked the little boy's logic. I watched as he looked up at his sister with a straight face, which made me want to laugh even more. I had a feeling that this was a normal relationship for the two of them.

"I know, but we have to wait a little longer for food."

Those two weren't the only ones hungry. I was starving too. I kept glancing at the two of them as they each swung from one of Lauren's arms. Lauren seemed tall next to the two of them. She always seemed smaller at school. Was it because we were always sitting in desks, not near each other?

"We'll walk over those hills and see if that town is up and functioning."

Lauren agreed by nodding her head as we

headed over the hills and I helped her with the two little ones when they almost fell. Once they were standing next to me, I helped Lauren by pulling her hand to give her some balance. Her hand was smaller than mine. It was strange seeing her long, clean nails against my hands. In school I never really noticed or thought of her.

Moving on, I quickly snapped out of it, and I helped the two girls. I really needed to learn the rest of their names. I doubted they would want to be referred by numbers. Cole didn't want any help, so I let him stumble over the rocks on the slant.

"Aaron, we have a problem," Lauren said.

I stared at her, confused, as I climbed the rest of the way to the top where she turned to look at me. My eyes went wide, and my jaw dropped, not believing what I was seeing. Only a couple of feet below us, water covered everything with only a few things sticking above the new water line. I thought I saw someone's satellite dish poking out. This was definitely not looking good. I turned right and left, seeing that the water stopped along the hills, but this couldn't stay forever. We had to move before it rained or something. It looked like the ocean had found its way to us.

"Aaron, does this mean the ocean was hit with one of the asteroids?" Lauren asked in a murmur near my ear.

I couldn't speak, so I just stood there, shaking my head and shrugging my shoulders in disbelief. This couldn't be happening. This was getting more awful by the second. Just when I didn't think things could become stickier, they did.

"Hey! Look, Paige. The beach came to us!" shrieked the little boy at Lauren's side, his hands shooting up into the air.

He was about to run over to the water, but I was able to grab him by the back of the shirt before he could make his leap. My heart almost leapt out of my chest. I wasn't sure how Lauren would react to see her brother dive into the wet unknown. Lauren grabbed him from me and held him close to her with her eyes closed tightly.

"Lauren, I can't breathe. You're hugging me too tight." The little boy squirmed in her embrace, using his small arms to try to push his sister away from him.

I smiled at the little guy as I picked up the little girl with dark red hair (who must've been

Paige) just in case she tried what he had failed doing. We really didn't need to any more attempts.

"Sean, you can't do that. You don't know how to swim. Stay by my side and don't leave me." She nearly cried, her hold on him didn't seem to loosen.

I was a bit taken aback by this. I had never seen anyone that caring over a sibling. I was adopted and didn't have siblings. I watched her practically killing her brother with her hug because the fear of losing him was too much to bear. I was resentful of them.

"Lauren, we should probably keep going," I said quietly, trying not to sound bitter and attempting to push those feeling deep inside of me.

"Okay."

We headed down the hill slowly, trying not to kill ourselves from the tilt. I kept a close eye on Lauren carrying her brother. Once we were on our way again, we changed our direction, so we were heading west.

"Lauren, what are everyone's names?" I asked, kind of embarrassed it took me so long to even ask.

She grinned. "This is my brother, Sean,

and the one you are holding is his best friend Paige... Both are six. The one that has black hair a little shorter than her shoulders is Jill, and the other girl with very short brown hair is Mandy. Then there's Cole, and you know me from school."

"What are the others' ages?"

"Cole is sixteen, Jill is fifteen, and Mandy is nine."

Nine wasn't too young, so the only ones we really had to worry about were Sean and Paige. They would need the most help and attention.

"So, oh dear savior, what is plan B?" called out a voice reeking of bitter sarcasm.

I turned to glare at Cole, stopping everyone in our little group.

"Listen to me you little piece of—"

Lauren slapped me on the back of the head. I felt so stupid, as I stood there in shock with my mouth left wide open. She hit me!

"Listen, you two! We have to get along if there's any chance for us to stay alive. One person alone can't survive out here, so we have to work together and stop fighting with each other. We don't know what's out there, so come on, please get it together. Furthermore, no cursing! There are little kids around us!" Lauren ordered. I almost felt like I was back at school with her scolding us.

I looked at the quiet bookworm who was now bossing me around and I couldn't believe I was desperate enough to save her. I knew that was horrible to think, but I could tell this was definitely going to be harder than I thought with this group. She marched ahead of Cole and me with the other two girls, as I stood there with the little girl in my arms. Paige glanced up at me with big, brown apprehensive eyes, almost desperate for any comfort she could get. I was not known for my reassuring traits or my child-caring skills; I didn't know what to do. I had to listen and work with the geek if we had any chance for all of us to survive.

"I'm tired."

"My feet hurt."

"Please! I don't think I can carry either of you anymore. I promise we'll stop soon," Lauren begged after hours of walking.

I knew we should have been close to Pennsylvania, as I remembered how long it took when my parents took that trip there two summers ago and we have been walking for hours. I glimpsed over at her and I could tell they were all as tired as I was. The lack of sleep was taking its toll on me. Except, unlike the rest of us, Lauren had the two little ones clinging to her, and they only wanted her.

Holding Paige didn't last very long as she was afraid of me, so Lauren had one on her back for a while, with the other in front. Then she made them walk for a bit. They wanted to be held again, but Lauren didn't have the strength at the moment. I honestly didn't know how she held the two of them for as long as she did.

"How about we take a little break then? We're not too far from the border."

I thought we were anyway. It was hopeful thinking on all our parts.

We still hadn't found a place that hadn't been affected by the water or the rocks to find people who were still alive to help us. So, we decided to go to Pennsylvania to see if anyone was there. I had my fingers crossed. Lauren practically collapsed onto the ground when I spoke of a break. The others followed her. How hard had I pushed them?

Lauren curled up on a small patch of grass by a tree. Sean and Paige soon pursued a spot next to her since she was the nearest thing, they had to a mother now. Sean was right against her as he held his friend close to him and then Lauren put an arm around both to keep them secure. Mandy was with Paige and Jill went along with her, leaving Cole to watch, sitting by a tree nearby. Then there was me, the misfit in the group, watching them.

I sat down, observing them and not certain on what to do. I knew I had to form a relationship with them since we would be together for a while. I couldn't figure out how to bond with this group so that we could work together. I mean, I wasn't up for playing house with Lauren. The new family in the works had Lauren as the mother... and me, well... the father of these kids. That just wasn't my style or part of my plan when I helped them out of the basement. I had only wanted to help them out of the wrecked house. And yet I felt the feeling of need to be with them.

"Lauren," the little girl's voice pipped up from the silence that had taken over.

"Yes, Paige?" Lauren mumbled, sounding half asleep.

"The scary man is looking at us."

"What scary man?"

Lauren sat up in alarm, and I scanned around. Then Lauren let out a small giggle as Paige started to point to me.

"Paige, that's Aaron. He isn't going to hurt you. You should probably take a small nap, okay?" Lauren aimed to soothe the girl in a tender voice, caressing the little girl's cheek as she lay back down.

Great. I saved their lives and I'm referred as the scary man. Not something any guy wanted to hear. I watched as Lauren kept the two close to her and hummed with her eyes closed. They seemed to fall asleep to her random tune, and I realized I was starting to smile. I caught myself and stopped the grin from showing for too long. I really wanted to be near them, but I couldn't let myself for some reason. There seemed to be a wall around me I wasn't willing to jump over. What was wrong with me?

After yesterday's break, we headed out early the next morning. No one seemed excited to be waking up to continue travelling, not that I could blame them. By how Cole acted, anyone would think that I did this stuff for fun. That was not the case.

44

Today the sky was gloomy. The clouds were pronounced in addition to slow moving. Yet the scent in the air was still smoky.

Lauren held the children by their hands, while they were trying to play 'I Spy.' Lauren was worried about playing that game because we didn't know what exactly we would find in the surrounding area. The last thing she wanted was a dead body to pop up.

"I spy with my little eye something that is gray!" Paige exclaimed with a wide grin on her lips.

Scrunching his face, Sean inspected the world around him.

"A rock?" he asked as we drew closer the shambles of buildings and stacked up boulders that used to hold up bridges and roads.

I glanced around for something that was gray.

"Broken building?" Lauren questioned; her voice somber, probably anxious that a six-year-old would pick that as her object.

Paige giggled.

"Nope! Lauren, you're wrong!" Paige squealed. "Do you guys give up?"

"How about you ask Aaron?" Lauren suggested, smiling as she peeked over at me.

I raised an eyebrow.

"What do you think it is?" Paige inquired; her voice not as happy as a moment ago.

"Um," I started not really sure what was gray around here. "Clouds?"

Paige giggled once more.

"Nopes! I win! It's a bridge!"

I looked up from our path to see a long structure before us. The metal pieces at the top were bent in parts, yet there was our chance to explore for safer surfaces. We approached the bridge, the Delaware River covered in small white caps from the now rapid-paced current of the river. Yet in the middle of the water, after what seemed to have crashed through the road of the bridge, was a smoldering asteroid. The heat of the rock and the cooling water cause steam to flow around the area like dry ice at Halloween.

"How are we supposed to cross that?" Jill asked.

"Hope there is still area for us to walk on." Lauren responded with a shrug of her shoulders, but doubt was written all over her face.

"Only one way to find out…" I spoke up, trudging in front of the others.

We were all next to each other, long ways, walking across the medal grid of the bridge. Our steps were cautious. There were cars abandoned along the bridge, burned up bodies in the driver's seats in a couple of the cars. The trapezoids that acted as tall metal, gapped walls of the bridge left faint shadows on the ground.

Once we reached the middle of the bridge, there was a hole that took up the bulk of the bridge, leaving only the perimeters to walk on, which tested our balancing skills. I put Sean on my back, and Paige clambered on Lauren's as we walked carefully—one foot in front of the other. Silence overtook us as rushing water filled our ears. I stopped myself from holding hands with Lauren to keep her close behind me. I held my breath, hoping that we would all be safe. I glanced up at the wooded trees before us. We only had to get through this section, and we would be out of harm's way for a while.

"Only a little bit farther, guys!" I yelled over the sound of the water.

The vapors from the asteroid made my eyes water. I felt Sean lean over on my back in order to get a better look at the rock that was related to the ones that ruined our lives.

"Try to stay still a little longer, Sean. We

are almost away from the hole. Once we get off the bridge you can go crazy."

He listened without a comment as he straightened up on my back. Lauren yelped just as I stepped onto the stable part of the bridge. Just in time, I pulled Lauren firmly against my chest. Her blue eyes locked onto mine.

"Let's keep moving before the bridge falls apart," Lauren spoke up before we rushed off the bridge and into woods, not knowing what was ahead of us.

Paige and Sean were running circles around us as Lauren and I were hoping that we were nearing a town. One that would be, well, not completely destroyed. Lauren kept an eye on the children; she seemed to be anticipating for them to fall as she kept her hands out, ready for action. So far, finding a safe place wasn't looking good, which worried us. Well, not the two little ones, who seemed kind of oblivious to the situation. I hadn't heard a word from Mandy and Jill since we woke this morning. They seemed to be in shock, but still, it's not like the rest of us weren't.

"When can we stop for food?" asked Cole, his voice sharp.

"We'll eat when we actually find

something to eat," I answered while watching the two youngest ones, trying to make sure I don't trip over them again.

"We haven't seen anything for hours," he growled.

"We did take apples off the tree," Lauren added, coming into the argument between Cole and me. Her eyes were on Cole.

She was now carrying a book bag I found, which must have been left behind by a camper. The owner was nowhere in sight, nor was there food in the sack. As we continued to travel, we came across a farm; parts were still in a haze from the asteroids. There were still some apple trees that were not completely destroyed. We picked some of apples to fill the backpack, not sure when we would find food again. The little two couldn't reach the trees were still eager to hunt down apples. We attempted to try to show them what a good apple looked like and what a rotten or an unripe apple looked like.

"I don't want apples," Cole grumbled. "I'm fine."

I wanted to hit him! Before I could get a chance to do anything, I felt something touch my hand. I turn to see Lauren pulling me along with her and the two little ones. This gesture was something utterly shocking from her, leaving me dumbstruck. She started to quietly walk along with me, as the two little ones then started to run circles between us, her long fingers interlaced with my own. Lauren laughed making it the first real amusement through this whole mess and I smiled. Maybe there was hope after all.

"I'm really looking forward to finding a town soon," Lauren spoke, changing the topic, sounding tired and a little down on her luck.

"Yeah, same here," I responded, looking down at our locked fingers.

"Not to sound high-maintenance, but I really want to shower," she continued, oblivious to the fact our fingers were intertwined.

I gave a small chuckle. We all didn't exactly smell like a basket of flowers at the current moment. I wouldn't blame anyone for wanting to shower, especially since it's been a few days since our last one in a real bathroom.

"It would also be nice to have an actual bed for them to take their nap."

"Yeah, I know what you mean. Hopefully, we'll be able to get you some shoes, too," I said, looking down at her bare feet, which were pretty dirty, and wishing not to find blood on them caused by all the rough terrain.

"Well, yeah it wasn't like I planned on needing shoes, so I took them off in the house. Just be happy that the others have shoes."

"I still feel bad about making you do all this when you don't even have any shoes on," I spoke, as her and I raised our arms up like a bridge for Sean and Paige to run under.

"We've been walking on grass, dirt, and the occasional puddle, so don't worry about me," she answered genuinely.

That was when some vapor started to rise in the air in the distance. We were drawing closer. I held my breath, fearing that we had come across another deserted town. A town which would be completely in ruins without a single sign of life. So, we approached slowly, not sure what to except. The town showed no signs of people but looked in decent shape. Most of the windows were broken, doors askew, and a couple of buildings looked unstable, but not too bad. We headed toward one of the houses with its door slightly open, but it was still connected to its hinges. Letting go of Lauren's fingers, I went in first, not sure what to expect.

"Hello!" I called into the hallway. My voice filled the rooms, bouncing back to us; the home almost had an air of hollowness.

When no reply came, I tried again. Still nothing. The rest joined me in the doorway, in a tight cluster. There was some dust on the floor, but the place shouldn't have had this much dust. Then I realized it wasn't all dust, but dirt. The area must have had a strong windstorm from the asteroids from our town and the winds from the new shoreline.

"I guess we should stay here for some rest?" Lauren asked.

"Yeah, but stay on the alert," I replied, still scanning the interior of the house. My adrenaline was ready to kick in.

Lauren watched as the two little ones separated from the huddle and started to jump on the couch in the room next to the door, then raced up the stairs, their feet thudding loudly. I was not sure where their energy came from. Lauren ran after them, not wanting them out of her sight. I stayed with the other three.

"We should check the house out and see if they still have food in here," I finally spoke, trying to break the silence that was filling the downstairs.

We went into the kitchen and saw the windows were wide open. I thought back to home, my dad was not happy with the electric bill, so he turned off the AC and had the windows wide open, allowing the fresh air to fill the house. Shaking my head, I brought myself back to the present. The refrigerator wasn't working, but the owners still had food in the pantry.

"Don't eat all of that now; you can eat a little now though. Cole, watch them and I'll go check on Lauren."

Cole mumbled something incomprehensible under his breath, so I ignored him, knowing it wasn't going to be good. I climbed up the stairs after the three to find them in the first bedroom. It seemed like it must have belonged to a child since there were a few toys in there that they were playing with while Lauren laid on the small bed.

"You want to hide here for a few days?" I asked the sleepy Lauren, her eyelids fighting to stay open.

"You think it's safe?" Lauren questioned.

"We hadn't run into Manson yet, so the odds are pretty good we'll be safe here."

"I wasn't just referring to him. If everywhere looks like what we've seen, if there are any people left, they're going to be desperate and kill anyone in their way."

"Don't worry about anything until we run into it. If we stay on our toes, we'll be fine. Just don't be Chicken Little and expect danger behind every corner," I said, trying not to make it come out as a snap.

She pushed some of the curly auburn hair, which had fallen in her face, behind her ear. Her upper lids eyes were falling heavily to meet the bottom ones even though she fought to keep them open. I watched her nodding off, then her eyes burst open blink furiously.

"How about you take a shower now since we don't know when the next time, we'll see one again? I'll keep watch."

She raised an eyebrow at me.

"You'll keep watch?"

My eyes went wide. Not what I was hinting at!

"Out here! I'll be out here... keeping watch over the little ones and everything," I spoke, nearly tripping over my words.

"Are you sure that is a wise move for me to do that?"

"Sure, why not? It's just a shower; then you can take a nice long nap or attempt to really sleep. You can even go see if the people in the house left anything for you to use. You could actually get shoes."

She stood up slowly and walked past me to the room next door to this one. I heard the door shut and water start. The other two turned to look at me, finally realizing that I was there, as if expecting me to entertain them. I was never great with kids. I never knew what to do with them or what to say. I usually had to watch what I said in front of them. My mouth didn't always have the best censor.

"You want to play with us?" asked Paige holding out a stuffed lion to me.

"Um…sure," I answered nervously.

I walked over, bent and took the animal, not sure what to do next. Thinking of what Lauren would do, I sat on the floor with them. I crossed my legs and sat the lion down to look at their dog and raccoon.

"Hello there, Mr. Dog. How are you?" I pretended to use a weird voice.

The girl let out a loud sigh of annoyance. Her eyes rolled dramatically.

"The lion is a king so he wouldn't talk to them like that. Haven't you ever seen *The Lion King*?" Each of her words were sharp and direct despite her age.

Yup. I was definitely not good with kids. I

really wanted Lauren to get out of the shower soon, so that I could take one. Actually, I think we all were going to try to take one. I hoped there would be enough water for all of us.

"Bow down to your king!" I tried again in a deeper voice.

"Oh, hale King Aaron."

They giggled. Okay I can handle them. This didn't seem so bad.

"Down with the king!"

Whoa! Down with the king?! How did we get to this? Then the two of them dropped their animals and jumped at me. They both attached themselves around my neck, knocking me down to the floor in complete surprise. Their laughter echoed through the house as they sat on my chest and stomach.

"Oh, you think that is funny, do you?"

They just kept on chuckling. They had knocked a seventeen-year-old male onto the floor. Being gentle, I flipped us over and started to tickle them, a hand on each of their tummies. Their hilarity and their pleas for me to stop rang through the house as they wiggled about. Their smiling faces as they giggled made me forget what had happened to our lives. A moment of escape from reality. That was when I heard someone else laughing.

I looked up at the door to see Lauren. She was out of the shower now and standing in a pink towel. Her hair hung loosely, soaking the rim of the towel, but it was still curly. One hand was holding onto the top of the towel and her other hand covered her mouth.

"Is something funny?" I asked.

I stood up and headed toward her. She still had the giggles and tried to stop them by biting down on her lips. It wasn't working and I looked into her blue eyes. A new feeling washed over me as I looked at the girl in front of me. I hadn't ever noticed her in this way; she was beautiful. It's easy to miss something when you weren't looking, even when it was right before you.

"I was just playing with them," I continued.

"I can see that. I also saw them attack you."

She was unable to hide her amusement, as her lips were almost to their limits.

"Are you ticklish like your brother?" I blurted out.

Her eyes widen in fear as her giggles stopped short. She held the towel tighter to her body.

"Sean, is your sister ticklish?" I
questioned without my eyes leaving Lauren's.

Sean got off the floor and walked up to
me. Lauren started to shake her head "no" to her
brother. He was grinning big and I could tell the
answer already.

"She is *very* ticklish. She's even more
ticklish than I am!"

Oh, this was too easy.

"Aaron, don't you even think about it!"
Her voice wavered.

I took a step closer with a big smirk on
my face. She took a step back and I had the two
little ones as my miniature followers. You didn't
have to bond too long with these two to win
them over.

"Get the big sis!" roared Sean.

Lauren squeaked as she ran toward the
next closest bedroom. Her long legs were
showing under the pink towel as she tried to
close the door, but the two were in her way. She
was not about to be rough with them.

"This isn't funny anymore! Can't you
wait until I get clothes on at least?"

Okay so the situation was a little unusual,
but very amusing, and we all needed a little

enjoyment. Any girl should know not to walk around a teenage guy with just a towel on and let him find out she's ticklish! I ran through the entrance as the two little ones had her cornered on the bed.

"Aaron, stop this!" she yelled, but there was a hint of laughter as she tried to be serious, so she wasn't thinking of me as a pervert.

The three of us closed in on her as I heard footsteps running toward the room. I so close to Lauren. I placed a hand under her chin as I drowned in her cobalt eyes. Slowly I drew her lips toward mine and the moment right before our lips touched a noise made us stop and turn to see what it was.

There at the door stood the other three with wide eyes. Mandy started to giggle, and Jill was blushing with wide eyes. Out of the stuffed-animal duo, one looked ready to join Mandy's reaction as Sean seemed to be ready to make the "ew" facial expression. Cole, with his fists clenched at his sides, looked angry. The more I thought about it, the more I realized something fast. Cole liked Lauren. I grinned at this fast recognition. Then I looked down at the toweled girl not even an inch away from me and couldn't believe what almost happened.

"What happened?" inquired Jill.

"There are fresh towels in the bathroom. Take short showers guys since we don't know how much water is still working in the pipes. Now, everyone out! I'm going to see if there are any clothes in here, I can borrow, then I'll give you two a bath in the other bathroom."

She shooed us all out, then locked the door quickly behind me after our eyes briefly met. Jill ran into the bathroom first, slamming the door in a hasty fashion. Mandy waited next to the door next while Cole just stood in the hall glaring at me. Yup, I was definitely right about him liking Lauren. Paige and Sean waited with me outside her door for a few minutes. And finally, the door opened.

She had braided her hair back tight and was now wearing a red tank top that didn't quiet reach the top of her jeans. The light blue jeans were ripped. It was apparent the girl who once lived here and Lauren were not alike or the same height. She held out her hands and the little ones took them as they left to go to another room. I got up and followed them.

Lauren started a bath for the other two who were wearing their bathing suits under their clothes. Lauren explained they were at a party when everything fell apart so this didn't surprise me. She sat on the edge of the bathtub as the water raised, and I watched her, not understanding my feelings toward about her. I mean, the other day, just being around her was irritating.

"So, I'll shower in here," I spoke up.

She turned around with her eyes wide. "What?"

"The line will go faster if we use what we can. It's not like you'll see anything anyway. The glass is distorted."

"Are you nuts?"

"Possibly," I responded with a smirk.

I have to admit it will be fun making her squirm. I walked over to the shower and started the water. She actually turned around with a look of pure shock and disbelief. I just smiled as I reached for the end of my black shirt and pulled it over my head. She was now looking the other way, twisting the knob ending the flow of water for their bath.

"So…" I paused. "You think wanting to put the clothes through the washer and dyer is pushing anything?" I asked after I got a whiff my.

I blinked a couple of times, dropping my

shirt onto the floor.

"I don't think so."

The two little ones in their bathing suits went into the water. They squealed as they splashed each other. I was resentful of them for having each other. Not angry with them, just jealous enough to wish I had someone with me too.

"Sean, when I said bath, I meant with soap!"

They laughed as I smiled, taking off my jeans and leaving them in a pile next to my shirt. I jumped into the shower and threw the boxers over the top. Lauren then left the room, not looking in my direction. Then she came back and went back to the bathtub. I finished up the shower, then grabbed the towel after opening one of the sliding doors a little. After I wrapped the towel around my waist tightly, I came out of the shower and stood by the bathtub as Lauren helped Paige wash her hair. She kept one hand near Paige's face to prevent the shampoo from going into her eyes.

"We'll wash everyone's clothes at once after they are all done."

She wasn't looking at me as I stood there in nothing but a towel and a half smile.

"Okay."

Lauren grabbed the two towels next to her as she tried to get them out. I grabbed one of them with the towel as they fought us to stay in the tub. She then pulled the drain, and the water went down, which forced them to get out.

"Come on. Let's see if the others are done."

She walked out of the room with Sean behind her, so I put Paige down and they ran ahead of us to the room with toys. Standing against the wall, Mandy and Jill were in towels, holding their clothes. Cole then came out with the towel around his waist. He looked at me, then down at himself and back to me again, conspicuously. I grinned at him as Lauren started down the stairs.

"Aaron can you keep an eye on Paige and Sean while we're downstairs?"

"Not a problem."

Hopefully they won't tackle me again.

I made my way back into the children's room. Their towels were long forgotten on the floor as they went back to their animals from earlier. This time the two weren't including me. I sat on the ground the best I could with the towel. I heard loud steps coming up the stairs and saw the girl with the dark skin and short black hair, I still couldn't figure out who Mandy and who was Jill.

"The electricity works!"

That was the little detail I forgot about when we talked about washing clothes. The electricity worked? I could have sworn the fridge was off.

"Are you serious?"

"Yeah Lauren put the clothes in, then the detergent, after that she cursed under her breath about not knowing if the electricity even worked, then Cole started it anyway... and it worked!"

"How's that even possible?"

"I don't know. I just know that's what happened!"

She ran back down the stairs to the others. I wanted to see if she was telling the truth, but I couldn't leave the little two for fear of what Mother Hen Lauren would do to me for leaving them. So, I stayed with them. I could feel my blond hair drying and I wanted clothes right away. I didn't want to spend much longer in just a towel. I didn't want to flash the little ones. A while later, I was hit with something. I took it off my head and saw it was my clothes. I stood up and passed Lauren in order to get changed.

I went back into the room that was connected to the bathroom where we gave the little ones their bath. It must have been the master bedroom. Quickly I got changed and laid on the bed. The sky was darkening so there was just a dim red glow coming in. Lauren appeared in the doorframe looking weary. Slowly, she made her way over and lay on the bed, curling up into a ball. Her eyes began closing as her head hit the pillow. She was always tired, and I hadn't noticed this, which caused my nerves to pick up.

"Are you feeling alright?" I almost didn't recognize my voice.

"Yeah just a little tired. That's all."

I just looked at her, trying to figure out if she was lying or not. That was when the two little ones, holding sandwiches, ran into the room and jumped on top of the bed. Lauren smiled as she gazed at them. Quickly they put the last bite of the sandwiches into their mouths then lay between Lauren and me to fall asleep, the stuffed animals tucked safely in their arms. I knew Lauren was deep asleep, so I went to go check on everyone else, deciding she needed the break. The two girls were in the teenager's room talking to each other as they were giving into the sandman's demands. Cole was in the room we hadn't gone in, which was right next to the one Lauren and I were in.

He frowned at me, then I went back to our room. The second I walked into the room, I saw the three of them were no longer awake. Lauren was still on her side curled up into a ball and the two little kids were next to her. There was just enough room for me in the spot I was in before on the king-sized mattress. Slowly, I unmade the bed, trying not to wake them and pulled the sheets over them. I lay under the sheets, looking at them. I guess there was a place for me in this new family after all. Slowly, I went to sleep, glancing over at them as we were all close together.

A gun shot was heard through the night, killing all the peace that came over all of us for the first time since the asteroids hit. I quickly got up to look out the window. My eyes tried to adjust to the darkness. I stood by the wall glancing out into the front yard. There were a few people in the street with torches. I recognized the first man with the gun. My heart raced as I looked over to the now awake Lauren and the younger two. The little girl was near tears as she clung to Sean. Lauren had gotten up swiftly to see for herself what was going on. I turned to Lauren and held her by her shoulders and our eyes locked. I didn't know how much time we had.

"Lauren, Mr. Manson's men are here. Stay calm and listen. I want you to grab the entire group and hide in this house. I'm going to run out through the back to so they will come after me, but I'll still have a head start. I'll lose them and come back here, but I don't know how long that'll take. I want you to stay here and only move if you have no other choice. If you leave, I want you to keep going west so I can find you. Give me a week though, please." I tried to keep my voice hushed and composed as uneasiness took over my body.

"Alright." Lauren appeared sickly scared as she agreed, knowing neither of us were happy with this plan or believed my stress-free approach to it.

She looked worried, but I needed to get these men away from all of them. My heart pounded, wondering if my plan would even work. I really didn't know where I would run to, once I left the house. Would she listen? Could I even get away and not get killed by the men? I still had my hands on her shoulders. I pulled her into a hard kiss, then ran out of the house, hoping this would work before either of us could react further. I dashed down the steps, skipping half them. My feet nearly slipped from under me as I raced to the back. Throwing the door open, slamming the rear door behind me I made as much noise outside hoping they would hear me.

3

Lauren

Quickly, I came back to my senses and
rushed Paige and Sean out of the room. The
other three were already in the hallway probably
curious about all the noise, so we piled into
Cole's room then locked the door. I really had no
idea what I was doing or should be
accomplishing, so we huddled together tightly
in the closet, just as we had under the table. I
couldn't hear anyone coming. We were in there
for a little bit before I came out to look out the
window. I saw the little lights move farther
away like dancing fireflies, so I knew the coast
was clear, at least for now. I let out a big sigh,
but suddenly now that the panic of getting
caught was gone, the fear shifted to fret over
Aaron's safety.

"So, where's the big shot now?" Cole's sour voice brought me back from gazing out the window to glance back at everyone who was still in the closet in a group embrace.

I turned to narrow my eyes at Cole, then went back to the window, biting my lip.

"He left," I answered quietly, wrapping my arms around myself, eyes still glued to the outside world, following the firefly-sized lights dancing in the distance, getting duller by the second.

"Ha, I knew we couldn't depend on him."

"He left to get the men away from us!" I snapped, my hands firmly on my hips.

I was angry at Cole for taking up that bitter-cheerful tone because Aaron was helping us. Cole had to stop causing fights between all of us. Aaron was trying to lend us a hand, and there was such a small amount of people left that we had to stick together. Aaron had done nothing but attempt to figure out what to do from the very beginning of this mess.

I grabbed onto the two little ones' hands and went back into the bedroom. They climbed back onto the bed without a single word, just soft yawns, after pulling the sheets over themselves. Hoping to fall back asleep with their new toys clenched in their arms, I looked at the children before getting in. I remembered falling asleep on top of the sheets. A smile spread across my lips knowing Aaron had pulled the sheets over us. I curled up under the sheets and fell asleep with the feeling of his lips against mine still fresh in my mind.

A few days later, we were eating breakfast, and from of all the worrying I had been doing, my stomach wasn't feeling well; my belly was in knots. I was one of those people who grew ill under anxiety. We hadn't seen or heard from Aaron for a few days, and I was growing restless. He was out there, and men with guns were chasing him. Aaron had no form of protection. On top of that, I had to take care of the five younger ones. I didn't know what I was doing. Even though two of the five were teens, I knew they were looking to me for signs that we were going to be okay.

"Just face the facts, Lauren, he isn't coming back!" A snarl brought me back.

I shook my head, wondering at first if that voice was my mind talking, trying to eat away at my sanity. Then I realized it was Cole. After finding out his parents were dead, he was taking the anger route of mourning. Not that I should judge how people react to the end of the world as we knew it.

"It has only been a few days," I mumbled. I rubbed my face. I didn't have the strength to keep arguing about this.

"It's been almost five days! If they got him, we're not far off their radar. We have to get away from here!"

"We have two more days!" I demanded, feeling in no mood for a debate over this topic. I knew I wasn't ready leave anyone behind.

Haven't we lost enough? Would we really become that close to suffering more?

"Why are we relying on him so much?" Cole shouted, which caused the little ones to first jump up, then sink lower in their shared chair. Over the last few days, they had become even more inseparable.

"He saved us!" I brought up; my voice did not come out evenly as I had wanted to make it sound like a pathetic excuse.

"We can keep ourselves alive well enough without him!"

"We're a team!"

"No! This isn't a team. It's Aaron the King

with you at his feet!" Cole's hands were in tight fists on the table so rigid that his knuckles were turning white and the muscles in his jaw tensed.

"That's not true because he's been helpful since he got us out of the basement in the first place!" I said.

"Why are we waiting for him? Is it because he kissed you?" he bellowed. "I saw him kiss you!"

I was stunned, my eyes widened to their limits. I couldn't think of what to say.

"He kissed you?" Jill squeaked; her dark eyes broadened with a matching smile.

"It was just a small one," I answered shyly, my fingers danced aimlessly on the edge of the table.

"You're so lucky! He's *so* gorgeous!" Jill squealed, her face glowing in excitement, showing what I had been trying to hold back.

"Hello, girls!" Cole's voice became more irritated, causing us to look back at him.

"How does he kiss?" Jill's eyes were gleaming with excitement. She was obviously eager for more information and obviously ignoring Cole.

"He is cute," Mandy spoke silently while making circles with her finger on the table, her cheeks having a touch of pink hue to them.

"Girls!" Cole nearly yelled, frustration seeping through the one syllable world. "Come back to earth and see the bigger picture! It doesn't matter how he looks or how he kisses. *We—have—to—stay—alive!*" The last few words came out slow and direct. Cole's face was red with exasperation as he stood up, his hands by his sides.

"I say we vote on whether we leave with or without Aaron," I finally said, though my mind was already made up, voting was just for show.

"That's not fair. You ladies have your minds made up already just based off his looks." Cole's brows were fused together, one slightly higher than the other, his head shaking slightly.

"Are you afraid?" Jill challenged, standing up next to me, just two inches shorter than me, but I wouldn't want to go against this athlete.

I thought back to all the night games of Red Rover and Man Hunt. Jill was competitive. She was picked before some of the guys.

"Remember, we have Paige and Sean to vote also," I brought up.

"They're six! You can't be serious!"

"We can vote!" shouted Sean as he stood up on the chair with his fists on his hips, eyes narrowing at Cole. His attitude didn't fit his little stature.

"They can't vote on something this important." Cole sighed, staring at me instead of my brother who was still glaring.

"Why not? Aaron probably would have let them vote," I answered unsure of that myself, my tone was steady though.

Cole frowned.

"*Fine*, they can vote."

"Who wants us to wait for Aaron?" I asked, glancing around the table.

Jill and I were raising our hands, but Mandy didn't budge as Cole's vision was fixated on Mandy.

"Mandy vote how you want and ignore Cole," I said sweetly.

"She doesn't want to wait. So, who else doesn't want to wait for Aaron?" Cole shot back.

Cole and Mandy raised their hands. Mandy was looking at the ground though.

"Sean, Paige, you guys didn't vote," Jill brought up, she bent over a little to get more on a level with the two, her palms were against the tabletop.

"We don't know what we're voting for," answered Paige, titling her head in a questioning matter.

"If we should leave the house now without Aaron, or should we wait two more days for Aaron to come here, then leave," I explained, hoping that it would sway their vote in my direction so I didn't look like a dictator.

"Was Aaron the guy that tickled us?" questioned Paige, her face scrunched.

"Yes, that was him."

I was smiling at that memory. The scene was engrained into my mind.

"I want to wait for tickle man!" Paige shouted, her face lighting up.

"I want what Paige wants!" yelled Sean, putting his hand in the air like Paige.

"Sorry, Cole, you lost." I shrugged.

Now let this be the right choice. I stood up and walked up the stairs to lay down on the bed in the master bedroom, leaving the others in the kitchen without an explanation or time for rebuttal. I looked down at the bed and then climbed into it, pulling the sheets up to my chin. I held them tightly in my grasp, after bringing my knees into my chest to drift off to sleep. I hoped I'd made the right choice.

After I woke up, uncomfortable in my jeans, I walked over to one of the dressers and opened a couple of drawers until I found something to borrow to sleep in. Pulling out the fabric, I saw it was still not what I usually slept in, but it would do. I found one of those nightshirts that ended around the knees that had some dumb sports team on it. I changed into it in the bathroom and left the jeans and shirt at the foot of the bed as I hopped back in. I kept an eye on Sean and Paige playing some game. I wanted to be more comfortable. With heavy eyelids I curled up on an angle to watch the little ones.

I stirred again when the two little ones crawled into bed beside me. I didn't remember falling asleep. I started to wonder what was wrong with me since I was sleeping the days and nights away. Sitting up, I brought the sheets up to cover the kids. I pushed one of Paige's braids out of her face and noticed the small smile on her lips that had grown. She was finally having a good dream instead of the routine nightmares. I then looked at my brother and gave him a small peck on his chubby cheek. That was when I heard a small creak downstairs.

Slowly I pushed aside the sheets and placed my feet as softly as I could on the floor. I got up and took cautioned steps out of the room. Moving as quietly as I could, I crept out into the hallway and noticed I was alone in the hall. No one else must have heard anything. Just as I was about to go back into the bedroom thinking I was hearing things, there was another creak from the stairs. I tried to squint in the dark. My heart raced as I feared Cole was right and someone was now after us, as I watched a shadow climb the stairs. I couldn't move out of fear, and the person was on the stairs growing closer. My hands began shaking.

"Hey."

I knew that voice! I jumped closer so I could wrap my arms around his neck, thanking God that it was Aaron and not someone who was out to kill us. I buried my face into the base of his neck as I felt arms envelop me, holding me close to his body. I've never been so happy to hug someone before in my life.

"If this is the welcome back I get for leaving, I should leave more often," Aaron whispered with a small chuckle in my ear.

"Don't even joke like that! I thought you were someone coming to kill us!" I spoke with my face still against the nape his neck, unable to let go of him.

"I told you I'd be back." His words were soft. His arms were still around me, and neither of us showed any signs of letting go.

"You also said you weren't sure if you would live," I said, my voice sounding small.

"I'm here okay, don't worry. We'll be on the move tomorrow. Come on, let's get some sleep now."

Relief washed over me as we tip toed back to the room. One of his arms was still wrapped securely around my shoulders, as he soothingly rubbing my shoulder. Aaron walked to the other side of the bed, his arm slipping away from my body and he kicked his shoes off so he could lie down only to have Paige crawl closer to him for warmth. I smiled as he fell asleep not minding Paige cuddling up against him. Then I crawled under the covers to fall asleep myself. I really felt harmony take over the house. Maybe there was a smile on my face like Paige's.

I finished exchanging the girl's clothing for my own. I left the girl's clothes on the bed minus the pants. I might need them when it gets cold out. I knew I couldn't wear my shorts forever. I bent over and picked up the backpack that was now filled with more stuff than before we came here. I ambled toward the stairs feeling kind of tired with a small headache starting to form despite the good night's sleep. I could finally sleep last night with everyone unharmed and under one roof. I put on the sweatshirt I was taking before descending the stairs.

"Ready to go, Lauren?"

I turned around to see Aaron heading over to me with the others. Sean and Paige were each taking a stuffed animal, so they had something to play with. I started to open the door as they filed out of the house and I took one last glance around the room. With a sigh I shut the door to join them. Carefully I took my time down the set of steps. My knees felt shaky, causing me to be a little behind the others. Aaron paused as the others leisurely kept on moving. I caught up with him. Aaron gave me a weird look; there was something in his eyes that I couldn't place.

"Are you all right?" Aaron finally asked me with a raised eyebrow, his neck craned o that our eyes would connect.

"Yeah, I'm fine."

Aaron just shook his head and looked

straight ahead. Aaron's eyes went to my shoulders before carefully taking the bag from me. With the weight off by back, I reached out for Sean's free hand. Aaron swung a strap over one of his shoulders and kept walking.

"I'm bored. Can we play a game?" inquired Sean, his little legs trying to keep up to our pace.

I glanced down at Sean and Paige, jealous of their energy. Sean always needed something to keep him busy; the games my parents made up for car rides for him were quickly made on the spot during times of desperation.

"Maybe later," I answered.

"Why not now?" he whined.

"We have to walk again. We're traveling right now."

"But that's boring," bellyached Sean, his shoulders rose just to fall.

"Lauren, when is my mommy and daddy going to come get me?" asked Paige as she held one of Sean's hands, her stuffed animal in the other.

I bit my bottom lip.

"Paige, how about we think of a game to play while we are moving to our next location?" Aaron stepped in, looking down at her.

"What kind of game?" Paige questioned; her head tilted to see him.

"Um, I don't know. Let's think of one," Aaron answered, taking hold of her wrist.

"How about… attack the big ape?" muttered Cole.

"Who's the big ape?" asked Sean, looking at Cole.

"Aaron is the big ape," Cole retorted with a smirk on his face.

"No, you're monkey poop!" yelled Paige, holding her toy tight to her chest as she turned around to glare at him.

I tried to laugh, but my head was still hurting, which was irritating my eyes and making me dizzy. To make matters worse, my stomach started to crawl up my chest. I was going to be sick. I tried to hide it all with a laugh so we could keep moving. I took a long, slow breath.

"A baby just insulted me!" Cole shrieked.

Aaron started to chuckle a little.

"I'm not a baby! I'm six years old!" Paige stomped her foot.

"Yeah, dude, get it right. Geez, what's your problem," Aaron joked with sarcasm that the little ones took as sincerity.

I giggled again feeling my head become heavy as the world around me whirled. I tried to calm my breathing, but it wasn't helping as my ears stopped picking up sound except a slight buzzing noise. Little gray dots popped up and blocked my vision. I don't know what happened next.

Gradually I opened my eyes and realized I was lying down on the ground, but I couldn't remember doing so. At a snail's pace, I tried to sit up. Where was I?

"Lauren, lay back down," an urgent yet soothing voice ordered.

I turned my head, which was still circling to see Jill walking over to me. Where were we? I don't remember walking around here.

"What happened?" I asked, placing my hands on my head to stop the spinning — holding the world in place.

"Just lay back down."

"I'm fine. Just tell me what happened." I started to sit up again.

She sighed. Jill's eyes closed briefly before looking back at me. "You fainted."

"I what?" I questioned, my eyebrows

fusing together. I didn't remember that.

"You were just walking and talking with us, and then you just fell. We couldn't wake you up, so Aaron had to carry you here."

The back of my head throbbed and the muscles in my neck ached.

I started to have that feeling again, the out-of-body light headedness. I lay back down, hoping it would keep the world from moving around me. I wrapped the sweatshirt tighter, as chills ran through my body, causing me to quiver. I closed my eyes as the world began to spin faster.

"Where's everyone else?" I asked, trying to stay in control.

"Mandy's watching Sean and Paige just over there, and Cole and Aaron went to look for better shelter nearby."

"Okay…"

I was already drifting again. I couldn't fight it anymore and darkness overcame me.

4

Aaron

Cole and I were heading back to where we left the girls in silence. The whole time, there was that thick air of awkward stillness between us. Was the silence better than the yelling? It didn't help that we wanted to kill the other at the moment. Finally, I saw Jill standing up not far ahead of us and picked up my pace a little. Jill was sitting by Lauren who seemed to be unconscious.

"How's she been?" I asked, bending down near Lauren to see how she was.

My eyes scanned Lauren's face. Her muscles were slightly tensed as she had a tight grip on her sweatshirt even as she slept.

"She was awake at one point not too long ago. She didn't remember fainting at all. Then I made her lay back down and she fell asleep instantly," Jill spoke evenly. I watched for signs of life with Lauren.

"If we walk a little longer, do you think you could carry Sean or Paige if you had too?" I enquired still looking at Lauren.

"Yeah, I could, why?"

"Cole and I didn't find much but moving somewhere else would be better than staying here in this wide-open space. I'll carry Lauren. Then if the two little ones get tired, you and Cole can carry them until we get to our next spot."

"Alright, that sounds like a good plan. Mandy, bring Sean and Paige over here. We're moving again," Jill yelled, waving the smaller three over to us.

"Why can't we stay here?" snapped Cole, causing me to turn my head up and glare at him.

"It's simple, Cole. Being in a wide-open area isn't the smartest thing to do!" I spoke, standing back up, slowly, the volume of my voice going up. "Especially considering all that's going on right now. It's like a suicide mission."

"That's only because we are letting a punk like you stay with us. We're only in danger because of you!" Cole growled.

I was so sick of this guy. My anger grew

with just one look at him. I restrained myself from taking another step closer to Cole as Sean stood next to me.

"Look here, kid, even if I wasn't with you guys, you would be in danger. We don't know what to expect out there. I know I'm not the safest person to be near, but I can still help. At least I keep you safe when I'm with you! So, suck it up and shut up, because no one wants to hear your tantrums fit for a two-year-old!"

I bent over and lifted Lauren and felt her shiver as if she were freezing. This was definitely not looking good. I moved Lauren in my arms a little so that she would be closer to my chest for warmth. We didn't have any medication other than the aspirin Lauren took from the house and I didn't think that would help with whatever seemed to be wrong with her. I could not even begin to guess what was making her sick.

"Come on, guys. Lets head out," I spoke, not really glancing at the others.

I started to march on with the two little ones beside me and Lauren in my arms still napping. The two girls were close to me with Cole a little farther behind, mentally throwing daggers at the back of my head. I didn't need to look behind me to know that. I could feel the flames from his eyes. He didn't care about what would help anyone but himself. That was the attitude that made me worry about what would happen later if he didn't change.

I glanced down at the girl in my arms. Her eyelashes were long and dark against her pale cheeks. Her pink lips stared up at me, I still couldn't figure out why in the world I would kiss them! The kiss was a question that ran through my mind when I was away. I mean, I didn't like her, so why did I grab her to kiss her! It didn't make any sense! Heat of the moment?

"We'll hide here under these trees for tonight," I finally spoke up.

Gently I placed Lauren down on the ground and I sat down next to her. It was too early to have one of us be lost, and if she was the first to go, none of the others would get through this.

There was no way that Sean and Paige would keep going if she died. They would die of broken hearts. They looked up to her like a mother, and if they knew their real ones were dead and Lauren fell to the same fate, there would be no real reason for them to keep going. If Lauren left us now, the little hope that there was would be gone. She shuddered again, so I brought her closer to me as everyone was falling asleep around us. Lauren's head resting on my chest, with my hands rubbing her back and arms in an attempt to warm her up. I would do anything to get her better.

"Are you kids morons?"

I bolted up after hearing someone bellowing. After I got my eyes to focus, I saw this old man standing there scolding us. He had white hair and a small white beard with beady brown eyes. He wasn't really that tall and had a beer belly that was stretching his worn-out shirt a little.

"What do you want?" I asked, hearing the snap in my voice. Closing my eyes for a moment, I pushed my hair back. I woke up too fast and was not ready to deal with another person.

"Well, apparently someone never learned manners!" His eyes were stern and focused.

"What are you talking about? You were the one who woke us up!" I glared at him.

"Well, it isn't my fault you kids are morons and went to sleep on the ground!"

"Well, last time I checked there wasn't a five-star hotel around here," I responded dryly.

What was with this guy?

"Shameful! Then to top it off you guys are teenage parents!"

"What the hell are you talking about?!" I really didn't get this guy, and what did he mean teenage parents?

I really did not have enough sleep in me to be woken up like this. I had no sympathy for him under those conditions.

"Those two little ones belong to the one sleeping in your arms!"

"That's her brother!" My voice sounded strange, stressed and shocked as it came out of my mouth, the words were quick.

"Sure, I'm sure that's what you just tell people! I'd get that red headed one checked though to see if she's really yours."

"Look here man—"

"No respect for their elders these days," the man said, shaking his head slightly, not in a rush to let me get a word in.

"Did you not take your medications this morning?" I asked with one eyebrow raised.

"You're a teenage parent and you're questioning me?"

"What is your problem?"

"My problem? I wasn't the one having sex on the ground!"

"I wasn't having sex with anyone!"

"Oh." His face relaxed, eyebrows rose looking at the ground. "So, you're in the doghouse?"

I just looked at this man shocked and aggravated. My mouth gaped, not sure what to say for a moment. Were the lights on and no one home?

"I'm not in the doghouse because I'm not with her. She's sick!"

"You got her pregnant again! What are with young people and having sex these days?"

"Young people and sex — that's all you have talked about to me, you crazy psycho!" I threw my words at him, a bite in each word, not able to hold back my rage toward him anymore.

"You can't talk to your elders about sex!"

"Why, that's all you have talked about?!"

"Yes, but it's my right as an elder, to do whatever I want!"

It was official; I didn't want to grow old if this was what was going to happen. I'll take dying young over this.

"You can't make up the rules as you go!"

"I'm an old man and you're on my property so yes I can!"

"Aaron…"

I looked down to see Lauren and the others starting to wake up. Apparently, our voices were rising without me really noticing. Her eyes were unfocused, and her movements were stiff; she was disorientated

Lauren spoke, "Sorry, sir, we'll get off your land."

She sat up slowly then tried to push herself off the ground. It wasn't working out too well for her. Lauren's arms shook and she wasn't able to get off the ground.

"Lauren, lay back down," I responded tenderly, trying to help her lay back down, which I could tell she didn't want to do.

"No. I'll be fine. This man wants us off his land." Her voice was hoarse, and I had trouble hearing her as she talked.

She finally stood up, using my body to help her to rise. She fell again, but this time I caught her. I held her close to my chest as she used my body as a crutch.

"I got you," I whispered in her ear, my head resting on top of hers.

"Is the girl alright?"

I turned to the old man, but he was kinder this time.

"She's sick."

"I'm fine, just tired."

"You're sick. Admit it, girly, before the jerk gets you into an argument. That would be a waste of energy in your state. My house is just up ahead. You all can stay there until you're better."

"Are you sure?" Lauren questioned; all her weight rested on me as her arms stayed around me.

"Well, the fact that you can't walk, and you have all these kiddies with you, I'm not lying. I don't lie to a lady, to jerky over here maybe, but not to you."

Just great, this guy was nuts. Not only was he nuts, but he was also only nice to girls. Please let this guy not be a sicko. We followed the man.

"Nut Job, do you have a name?"

"Aaron, be nice!" Lauren disciplined me from my arms. She sounded a little angry, but mostly drained with her head on my shoulder.

"Yeah, Aaron, listen to the little lady. My name isn't Nut Job by the way, it's Ed."

"Thank you very much, Ed," Lauren said

politely, her voice was weak.

"You may stay until the time is right."

We saw his log cabin-like home just a couple of feet up ahead, which didn't seem to have been touched by this whole disaster. He climbed up the stairs and held the door open for all of us to get in.

"You can put her down in that room, it used to belong to my daughter."

I started to feel bad for the guy right then and there as I walked into the room, placing Lauren down onto the bed. I was a real jackass.

"I'll be right back," I whispered as she started to close her eyes while attempting to get comfortable.

As I was walking out, the two little ones passed me to go into the room to be with Lauren. Cole collapsed onto the couch while Jill and Mandy were on chairs in the same room. I went into the kitchen to find the man.

"Thank you for this," I spoke with difficulty because I so didn't want to apologize to him. My voice was softer than earlier, but still stiff.

"You're the boy they're looking for, aren't you?" Ed asked, looking me dead in the eyes, making sure I was paying attention to him.

I raised an eyebrow.

"What are you talking about?"

"There was a man who stopped by here the other day, by the name of Dean Manson. He said he was searching for this boy and if I saw him to call the number on the card. He claimed his phone still worked. He kept talking about how he wanted this boy. He had a bone to pick with this boy."

I let out a big sigh, then turned to gaze out of the window. If Dean Manson was spreading the word, I was doomed. I didn't think I could find the words.

"I thought so. You're safe here," Ed said, knowing what my pause meant.

I looked back at the man shocked.

"Are you serious? Then why did you give me a hard time back there?" I inquired. My eyes ready to fall out of my head from how wide they were.

"Several reasons. One, I had to see if you were the boy. Two, to find out why you were with the girl and children since the man didn't mention them. Three, I had to make sure you weren't a spineless coward, and finally, I was bored," Ed answered nonchalantly with a shrug of his shoulders.

I let out a snort out of disbelief.

"Now go to sleep in that room with her," Ed said, before continuing. "Also, I have one rule if you are to keep on eye on her."

"Which is?" I asked even though I had a feeling I knew what he was going to say next.

"No sex."

I just rolled my eyes knowing I was right. What was with this man and sex?

"Trust me, that will *not* be happening," I responded, rolling my eyes.

"Are you gay?" Ed asked, very straight forwardly.

"No, why?" I was taken aback by this and I didn't have a problem letting him know this by my tone.

"You have a beautiful young lady, and you won't have sex with her."

Hanging around this man made me want to smack my head against a wall—a nice big thick brick wall.

"What happened to no teenage sex?"

"Eh, just testing you."

"Yeah," I spoke trying to keep down the frustration. "Night, Ed."

I walked out of that room before Ed could say anything else. With Lauren, Paige, and Sean on the bed, there wasn't room for me. There was barely room for them, so I sat on the chair in the corner of the room to fall asleep. It might not have been the most comfortable, but it wasn't the ground. I looked over at the three of them snuggling together. I missed the bed in our last place. It was comfortable and we were able to stay close together.

"Boy, how stupid are you? The girl is sick, and you put the little ones near her! We don't know how sick she is!" Ed's voice screeched. "They could get what she has!"

This guy sure knew how to wake someone up. I stretched and went over to him. My muscles felt like they had just been sprayed with hairspray because of how stiff they were.

"What is it now?"

"You don't know what is wrong with the girl, so you have your two little kids with her?!"

"First of all, they're not our kids! Secondly, I don't think I could separate them."

"And you call yourself a man! Kids, there's a working TV out here!"

That got them off the bed and running into the other room.

"Ed, do you know why some of the electricity works?"

I turned to see Lauren awake. Her eyes were half opened, but she was up.

"No, I'm just as surprised about it as you are."

He sauntered out of the room, so I went over to Lauren and sat at the end of the bed. The room fell silent without Sean and Paige.

"Ed thinks we better keep Sean and Paige from you until you're better, so they don't get sick," I started, watching her carefully.

"That might be wise..." Her voice was light as she was unable to look at me.

"How are you feeling, Lauren?"

"Not better, but before a storm passes, it has to get rough first."

"What?" I asked. Was there something about this house that made people crazy?

"Before a storm goes away, it has to get dire first. It will go away soon basically."

I just nodded my head. Why couldn't she have just said that in the first place?

"Are you sure about this Ed guy?" I asked with a raised brow.

I was really not sure about him, but it didn't seem like he was going to rat on me. I was curious as to what she thought of him despite the short time. I thought he was a nut and there was no question about it.

"He seems…" Lauren paused; her eyes went to the ceiling searching for the word. "Colorful, nice, and is giving us a place to stay, so how can we argue?"

She had a point, but I wanted to keep an eye on him anyway. How did I know I could trust him to not call Manson? I wasn't going to worry Lauren with that fact though. He could be calling him as I sat there with Lauren, who was hopefully not on her death bed. She started to tremble again as she buried herself in the covers. I really felt bad for her.

"Let me help."

Her sapphire eyes appeared confused and scared at the same time. I squished myself next to her on the twin bed under the covers, so I was lying on my side very close to her on the bed. I brought her shivering body secure to mine. Her skin felt like fire against mine and I couldn't believe she was quivering from the chills. Her back was alongside my chest as I wrapped an arm around her.

"Why are you doing this?" she asked through chattering teeth.

"We need you to get better. If it means body heat, then so be it."

"Thank you." Her weak voice sounded so sincere, just like how my foster parents used to speak.

"Hey, don't worry about it."

I felt stupid about not really noticing that she was getting sick as I back tracked through all her signs. She was always tired. She hadn't been really eating and I just took it as a girly thing, but she was getting sick. Even if I was never her friend, I should have noticed the signs as a human being.

I felt her breathing take a smooth out as she fell asleep. I lay by her side as the day not wanting to leave her. I got comfortable next to her as I fell asleep by her side myself.

I had spent two more days just like that one, lying in bed with Lauren and she didn't show any sign of getting better, which made that night very difficult for me.

Lauren had her head on my chest near my shoulder. My head rested on top of hers, as my fingers were absent-mindedly stroking her back. My own eyes barely open themselves, letting the laziness take over my body.

Ed came into the room and I opened my eyes at the sound of his footsteps. He tapped on my arm to get me up. I shifted Lauren, placing the pillow where I had been. Before I could get fully out of bed, Ed dragged me out of room. His eyes were wide. I was about to yell at him as he pulled me aside into the kitchen and started to talk, looking worried.

"Manson's men are coming. Before you start pointing fingers, it wasn't me who contacted him. The plan is that you hide somewhere else. I'll take care of them here."

I glanced over to where Lauren was.

"I can't leave her now; I think she's getting worse!"

Ed took hold of my shoulders and snapped my concentration back to him.

"Boy, that man is a powerful one! He has followers, not only from the few that survived in Jersey, but other states. He is picking up speed of support from the few that are alive, and he has weapons."

I was so ticked off at myself for getting into this whole mess with Manson. I looked at the bedroom that Lauren was in once more. I cursed the day that I sent Manson to jail. Why couldn't I have just stayed home instead? That moment of heroism was now putting others in danger.

"I hate doing this," I stated, not moving my eyes away from the room that I was in just a minute ago, my body felt rigid with dread.

"I figured as much," he said in a caring voice.

"I really don't want to run away." Anxiety continued to take over.

Not again. I did not want to run off on the group once more.

"It's for the best, for the kiddies," Ed spoke softly.

"Damn it!" I cursed under my breath.

"Go, boy! You have to leave before it's too late!"

"I really don't want to do this," I said finally looking at him, heart pounding.

"You're not a coward when it's the right thing to do."

Knowing he was right; I ran without another word. I left through the back door, not really sure what to do, but knew I had to get Manson's men on a new trail so I could go back to the group. I made trees rustle as I was going and stopped dead in my tracks. Manson and his men weren't following me at all. What was I going to do? Run or help the others?

5

Lauren

I gave a small shiver as I felt the bed move, my heat source was leaving my side. I turned over to see Ed pulling Aaron out of the room. I tried to sit up and wished I could follow them to hear what they were talking about. I wanted to be back in the decision making rather than being helpless, waiting for others to make my choices for me. That was when I heard a door open then close quickly. I began to worry since the last time there was rushing involved meant that someone was after Aaron, that night of the gun shot came back in whirl of a memory.

"Ed!" I cried out softly.

Ed came into the room looking frazzled.

"What's going on?" I asked feeling my whole body being taken over by my terrified nerves, even though deep down I already knew what was wrong.

"The men are in just a short distance from the door. I don't know why they returned here."

"What men?"

Please, intuition be wrong!

"Mr. Manson's men!"

"Oh God, Aaron!" I yelped, wondering where he was and what was going to happen to us.

"I already sent him on his way and he'll be back later on when the coast is clear. I hid the others in the attic. They're going to want to come into the house and I can't hide you because of your condition. If they ask, you are my daughter Tammy, okay?"

I just nodded my head looking into his dark eyes as there was a knock on the door. He left the room then came back with a few men. In front was a man that I instantly recognized just like Aaron said I would. Here was a man who was not fat but was a solid individual. He was about six feet tall with scowling gray eyes that seemed to be interrogating you the second upon making eye contact. On most of his face, he had a short dark brown beard. His hair was the same color and was cut rather short.

"Sorry Tammy, but these men just wanted to know if we saw a boy here," Ed spoke, standing aside for the cluster to come into my room.

"A boy, in my room? You know I don't do that, Daddy."

I tried to look at Ed, but Mr. Manson wouldn't let go of my eyes. He was holding my eyes hostage. His eyes were the color of storm clouds, fierce, locking onto me.

"You haven't seen a boy around seventeen and this height," Mr. Manson asked using his hands to about Aaron's height. "He has blond hair and blue eyes with a smart mouth on him."

"No, I haven't. It's just been Dad and I here. I've been sick, unable to even get out of bed." Well some of what I said was true.

"Is that why we didn't see you last time we were here?"

"I've been really sick and I'm just starting to get better. Dad is so overprotective and doesn't want the outside germs to make me worse."

I hope I sounded sincere and wasn't stumbling over my words. Trying to hold back the urge to chew on my lip, I swallowed back my fretfulness.

Mr. Manson just looked at me as if trying to figure out whether or not what I was saying was true or not. That was when there was a loud noise from outside, causing me to jump a little in my bed.

"Manson, I'm over here!" a shout came from outside the window.

My eyes went wide; then I quickly caught myself and held back the apprehension that I knew must have shown so he wouldn't think that I knew whoever made that noise. Dean Manson could not find out that I needed the source of the shouting to stay safe.

"Men, we're out," Manson spoke even tone, yet his eyes were still on mine.

Quickly they left without another word, leaving Ed and I alone in the room.

"That man of yours is crazy," Ed said, breaking the silence.

"Crazy he is," I said almost in a whisper. "Mine, he isn't."

I stared out toward the window, making sure I couldn't see Aaron in the hands of Mr. Manson and his men.

"I'll get you some soup after I get the rest out of the attic."

I just nodded my head, my eyes glued to the window. I really wondered if he would return. I slid down into the bed to look out the window, wanting him to come back. That was when it hit me how pathetic I was acting. We really didn't care for each other in the sense of love, but he did kiss me. He was probably just afraid he was going to die. It wasn't like there was a repeat of the kiss, and we hadn't even talked about that moment. Argh, when did life get so complicated? I mean, shouldn't these stupid problems just go away after a month of handling the much greater issues that have come to us? However, given our situation, the thought of losing another person was painful.

My legs were a little shaky but were happy as I walked toward the kitchen a few days later. Just the thought of being out of bed put a smile form on my face. Sean and Paige were sitting on high stools by the counter as they were eating something. I came up behind them and hugged them as they laughed.

"Lauren!" Paige's happy voice rang out as she wrapped an arm around me as Sean did the same.

"We missed you!" Sean nearly cried into my shoulder.

I kissed the top of both of their heads. I brushed my brother's hair off to the side.

"I missed you both. It's nice to be feeling healthy again."

"Hey, Lauren, you're back to the land of the living."

I turned to see Cole walking over. He was running his fingers through his brown hair with his bluish green eyes appearing a bit kinder than usual since Aaron wasn't around. His eyes had the same gleam that used to be seen in them.

"I'm happy to be out of bed," I responded.

"So, are we staying here?" Cole asked.

"What?" I was completely shocked.

"Are we going to be staying here with Ed?" he repeated.

"We can't impose on Ed forever," I answered, the grin left my face.

"I like Ed. He reminds me of a grandpa!" Paige giggled.

"I like it here too, but I don't think Ed had planned on keeping us forever," I replied, looking down at Paige who was pushing small stray of hair behind her ear. She kept her head tilted so she could look at me.

"Girly, loosen up. You're too young to get wrinkles," Ed said as he came into the house with a stack of wood in his arms, Jill trailing behind him with some of her own. "You kids can stay here for as long as possible. I'm not kicking you all out."

I was a bit taken aback by this. "You mean you wouldn't mind us living here?" I asked, having to make sure that I was hearing Ed right.

"I would take it up with Jerky, but I wouldn't mind."

"Is Aaron back?" I was surprised and felt cheerful about hearing this as I tried to hush that feeling down on the inside.

"Of course, he isn't back!" barked Cole. I turned to look at him, my eyebrow raised.

"I might call him Jerky, but stop the attitude," Ed ordered.

I turned to glare at Cole, so he went further into the kitchen.

"It has been a few days and I haven't seen him," answered Ed delicately.

I bit my bottom lip again, hoping he was all right. Aaron was fine last time.

"He might be a jerk, but he can protect

himself as long as he keeps his mouth closed. Then, he's in trouble."

I beamed weakly knowing that Ed was probably right. Aaron's sarcasm would be the death of him.

A few more days passed, and we were still with Ed. Jill and I each sat on a couch to read... Well, Jill was reading, and I stared blankly at the book trying to make out the letters since I didn't have my glasses. The last time I saw them was when we were back at my house before the asteroids. Paige and Sean were on the floor with Mandy, coloring in some coloring books Ed found in the attic from when his grandchildren came to visit. Cole was in the kitchen with Ed when there was a knock on the door. We all looked up not sure how to respond. We couldn't think of anyone who would be knocking. Ed walked over quickly then looked through the peek hole to turn around staring at us with wide eyes.

"Lauren take everyone up to the attic and stay there!" he spoke quietly, but firmly.

I became worried, but he gave me a look as I rushed everyone into the attic. We rushed into Ed's bedroom then into the attic. We hurried up the stairs. When we got up there, I shut the door behind us. We had the two little ones continue their coloring so they wouldn't notice the change of tone in the air. I found it was easy to distract them.

"Well good evening, men. What brings you back here?" Ed's voice came through as he opened the door.

I listened to what was happening, simultaneously happy and dreading for having thin walls. My body was stiff, anxious about what any movement would do.

"We still haven't seen that boy," a voice asked evenly.

"You would think a teenage boy would be easy to find," Ed spoke with ease.

"You would think so. Now you must be thinking why we are continually coming back here," answered Mr. Manson with his strong voice.

"I was in fact wondering why you and your men were doing just that."

I could feel the smirk on Dean Manson's face grow through all the wooden boards.

"Stay here. I'll be right back," I whispered to the others.

I went out of the door before they could stop me. I had to save Ed.

"We believe that either you and or your daughter are helping this boy."

"Now why would you believe that? My daughter and I live a quiet life away from the city. We keep to ourselves and don't do any harm to anyone," Ed defended.

I noticed that I left the bottom door opened a crack, so I peeked through, watching men with guns stand near our friend Ed.

"We believe that the boy was here."

"I wouldn't keep a teenage boy here with a teenage girl! Too many bad things could happen."

"Where is your daughter now?"

"She is finally feeling better, so she went out to see if the flower patch was still alive by the river."

Manson nodded his head as if he cared.

"I see, and how would I know if you were lying to me?"

"I have no reason to lie. I don't know the boy," Ed answered, his head following Manson.

"Here's the thing. We don't know who the girl is, but we know she isn't your daughter. Your daughter died in an apartment fire three years ago with her family. So, it does make me wonder what more you are hiding. I don't like being lied to."

My eyes widen as the men encircled Ed. I was about to open the door to help him. He needed my help! Ed lost his own family and was now being forced to suffer because he chose to protect us. I couldn't just stand here and watch him get hurt. I gripped the handle. I was suddenly pinned against the wall. I was about to yell at the person when I saw the body against mine was Aaron.

I turned to see how Ed was doing just as one of them put a gun to his head. I couldn't take my eyes away as the evil man pulled the trigger. A loud echoing filled my ears. Tears streamed down my face as I watched Ed fall to the ground, a pool of dark blood forming by his head.

"Split up and check the grounds to see if they snuck out, then we'll search the house in case he's here," Manson ordered.

Manson just kicked Ed lightly by his feet to see if he would move. Ed didn't budge. Ed who had taken in seven children he didn't know. Ed who had given us shelter even though I was sick, and he knew Dean Manson was after

Aaron. Ed who had taken care of us. More tears fell as Manson took a quick glance around the room then left slamming the door behind him with the house still shaking in his aftermath. After the door was closed, I pushed Aaron away hard and ran over to Ed.

I collapsed by Ed's body, not believing he was dead. Even though we didn't know each other long, Paige was right, Ed was like a grandpa in an odd way. I covered my eyes not able to look at him with the puddle of dark warm liquid around his head. I felt tears fall from my eyes and through my fingers.

"Come on, Lauren. We'll leave through the attic window where I came in. We'll do that so the rest of the group won't have to see this," Aaron whispered tenderly.

I didn't move. I was not sure if I could move.

"Lauren?" Aaron spoke again, putting a hand on my shoulder.

That was when I snapped.

"This is your fault!"

I stood up swatting his hand away from me. I tried to stand up straight in attempt to match his height.

"What are you talking about?" Aaron

asked with brows that met.

"He is dead because of you!"

Aaron looked taken aback by this. "Last I checked I wasn't the one who put the gun to his head!"

"No, but you might as well have been! Those men were after *you*! They killed him because he was protecting *you*!" I howled, furious and heartbroken.

"He told me to run!" Aaron countered.

"And you did! You just ran to protect yourself!"

"I was protecting you guys!" His voice sounded a little weaker that time. "I didn't want to. Ed told me to run…"

"Well you sure as hell did a good job with that! They killed Ed because of you!" I spat at him, not caring what his eyes showed.

"Well, Lauren, if you don't remember, you wouldn't be alive if it wasn't for me, either!" he yelled after getting a second wind.

"If you are going to keep using that as an example—"

"What? What could you possibly do to me?" His hands tightened into fists by his sides as he glowered down at me.

"How do I even know he won't kill one of

us because of you?" I threw at him.

"I won't let that happen!" he barked.

"You couldn't save Ed! He took care of us when you left! We lost someone who, in a short time, became a part of the family! We lost someone else, but this time it was because of you!" I hurled the words at him, hoping they would hurt him like I was hurting.

"Shut up, Lauren. You don't know what you're saying!"

"I know what I am saying. Stop undermining me! I might not have muscles like you, but at least I don't have people's deaths on my conscience! There's no blood on my hands! I hate you!" I screamed, hearing venom shoot through my voice.

"Well you're not high on my list, either!"

"Then stop 'helping' us and leave us alone!" I screeched, using my hands to aid with the air quotations.

"You wouldn't last five minutes out there without me!"

"We could and can!" I shouted, restraining a foot stomp.

"Fine, I'll leave you guys! See if you guys even make it through the night!"

"Fine!"

I felt the tears form, but this time they were tears of anger. I refused to give him the pleasure of seeing them fall. I bolted up the stairs into the attic and saw Aaron left the ladder by the window, which I guessed was how he got up there in the first place. Without saying much, I made the group go down the ladder, confused about what was going on. We left the house in silence. Not one of them asked where Aaron was and why we left without him.

Not long after that, we were near some wooded area. I decided that we should stop as I felt that my heartache from the events today take its toll on my body. My heart was actually in pain. I curled up into a ball that night when we were all ready to sleep and held back my tears until everyone was asleep. Once I started crying, there was no stopping. I wrapped my arms around myself tighter, as I sat back up and leaned against the tree trying to muffle my sobs. I bent over so my face was against my knees and I wished I was home with my parents. I wanted to jump into their arms so they could hold me as I cried on their shoulders. That was not an option now. Not only were they dead, but so was Ed. Not only were they dead, but I had chased away Aaron. I couldn't handle anymore loses.

6
Aaron

I hung my head low as I heard Lauren run past me. Closing my eyes, I listened to them all climb out the window. I know I shouldn't have let her get to me, but her words echoed through my head, seeping into my gut. Was it really my fault that the old man was dead? I looked at him, the still body surrounded by a pool of dark liquid. The old man and I might not have seen eye to eye, but I never wanted him dead. Ed didn't deserve this. There was no way I was going to let anyone else die because of me. I had to protect those kids, and most of all, I had to save Lauren from whatever else was out there.

I refrained from glancing back at Ed, fearing that I would see someone else lying there lifeless, just as Lauren's words had hinted. I scanned around the room just in time to notice Cole's back as he followed the others. I didn't even have to think twice about what I was supposed to do. I kept to the side and began to stalk them. Even though Lauren didn't want me around, there was no way I was going to leave them unguarded. We had journeyed this far, sticking together despite how hard life had been. There was no reason for us to separate now.

The group walked for a little bit then they stopped by some trees to rest for the night. I sat by another batch of trees until everyone had fallen asleep. I had to stay with them, so once they were awake, I would return to them, despite Lauren's words.

The next morning, Lauren woke up, looking like she hadn't really slept, which I hadn't done either. I was too worried to close my eyes. Slowly, she got up and walked to the creek nearby, which I hadn't realized was there. She took her shoes off as she slipped her feet into the water against the rocks. Lauren wouldn't lift her head, nor did she have the small smile on her face she normally wore. She began to move her feet a little, never making an attempt to elevate her head from facing the water. She plastered on a fake smile when Sean walked over to her.

I really didn't want to see her like this: upset and faking her happiness. I didn't think I could go over to her, not just yet anyway. She wouldn't let me talk to her and I knew it. It didn't take a genius to realize that. She took long, slow steps to the others and woke them up. They then headed farther into the woods. I had to stay a good distance away. If Sean or Paige saw me, they would blow my cover.

When they stopped for lunch, I noticed something was wrong. There was movement in the distance. I stood up and watched as two men drew closer to the group. I was ready to come to their aid in a heartbeat. There was not a chance that I would sit back and watch something bad happen to them.

"Well, looky here, buddy, a collection of kids." A strong, sly voice came through the trees.

"Yes, a nice-looking group of kids," a raspier voice answered.

They started to get closer to the group as Lauren and Cole hid the younger ones behind them. I felt my hands recoil into tight fists at my sides as I walked a little closer myself to them, yet I made sure that I was hidden behind the trees. I really did not have a good feeling about the two men and the way they hovered.

"I really like how this one looks," one of them said, his ravenous eyes not leaving Lauren.

"Get the hell away from us," Lauren shot back angrily, her eyes glaring.

"Where are your manners, little girl? A beauty like you should have fine manners." A voice that was strong attempted a low and alluring tone.

"You should be very nice to guys like us," the raspy voice continued for his friend.

The rage grew within me.

"Go to hell!" Lauren growled.

"What did I say about manners?" the strong sly voice seeping with fake politeness asked, as if he had manners of his own.

"Such pretty blue eyes and lips you have, girly."

"I think her legs are nicer, if you ask me," said the one with the raspy voice. His gaze fell to Lauren's legs then stayed.

"Leave us alone or —"

"Or what, girly? Is this guy going to hurt us?" He nodded toward Cole with a grand grin on his face.

Cole made no noise.

"No, but I will." I finally came out, voice steady.

I stomped over to them not able to hide anymore. Lauren appeared completely shocked as I stood by her.

"Awe, how cute. Prince Charming is coming to the rescue of the fair maiden."

"Leave them alone," I snarled.

"Or what, you'll hurt us?" The strong voice chuckled.

"Yeah, pretty much."

I walked over to them. The guys didn't flinch, and I started to wonder if I really had a plan. Why did I keep getting myself into these situations without thinking them through? Nothing, absolutely nothing, came to my mind as I stared at them. One was bigger than me and the other was about my size. This was definitely not going to be a fair fight. Cole sure as hell wasn't about to step in to help me.

"What are you going to do?" the stronger one asked.

I had no idea what to do. I couldn't think of how to go at them. One of the guys went to hit me, so I ducked only to get hit by the other guy. When I landed backward, I heard a girl scream.

Lauren? Thinking back to what one of my friends taught me when we were horsing around, I knocked him over by a swift motion of my foot so that it collided with his legs. He went flying as I stood up swiftly to punch his friend in the middle of his face.

"Get the hell away from us and leave us the fuck alone!" I yelled.

The two men looked at each other as if they were debating whether they should or shouldn't go. There was a moment of silence. The only sounds were my racing heart and rapid breathing. It seemed the two men were having a conversation with each other telepathically. Then the bigger one started to smile and let out a small snigger.

"We'll be leaving now, but don't worry. We'll meet again." The bigger one laughed with his strong, cunning voice as he looked over my shoulder at something past me. I turned my head to follow his gaze, wanting to know what he was staring at.

My knuckles were clenched as I saw what he was so interested in. Lauren. I loathed the look in his eyes—desire and possessiveness.

The two men left, all beaming smiles. I had a bad feeling about this. I watched them as they made their way back into the thick woods. I took a few deep breaths when I couldn't find them amongst the trees then turned around to look at a bunch of wide eyes that stared at me.

"What?" I asked.

"What are you doing here?" Lauren questioned and I couldn't read her face or voice. I felt guilty beyond belief when I only saw pain after looking in her eyes.

"I came back," I answered as I attempted to read her expression.

She just looked the other way then back at me. There were haunted shadows in her blue eyes.

"Can you and I talk for a minute?" she asked quietly.

She wasn't yelling so that had to be a good sign. Yet I still felt self-conscious at that moment I could tell she was feeling the same way. One of her arms was behind her back, with the other gripping her elbow.

"I agree, but we should keep moving so that we can get away from here before they change their minds and come back for us. I promise, Lauren, that we'll talk tonight though."

Lauren unlocked her arms to take the little one's hands before she made her way to start the trail as the others followed her lead. We were silent the rest of the day. Well, noiseless except for the happy chatter of Sean and Paige, who never seemed to be affected by what was going on. The two held Lauren's hands and began to swing them back and forth while they sang.

I could not believe the progress we made that day, but we had still not found anyone. We knew we were finished, however, when the little ones said so. I wasn't about to have Lauren carry one again for long because she still needed to recover. I didn't know how long she had been well since I came back, and I wasn't ready to test her health.

Lauren made dinner. She managed to make sandwiches from some of the food we found in her backpack, which was low since we were at Ed's and did not see a reason to restock. When everyone was falling asleep, Lauren folded her legs and slipped them under her sweatshirt. I walked over and sat down beside her. She didn't even turn to look at me.

"Are you ready to talk?" I inquired softly; my fingers rubbed against each other.

"Yes and no," she whispered automatically like a shell of a human being set on autopilot.

"I understand, but we need to talk about it now rather than later, so the argument doesn't distract us from surviving," I spoke tenderly.

I had never been in such a rush to actually talk out a problem before, especially with a girl.

"I know, but how do we even start?" she asked. Her voice was low, trying not to wake the others. Her hands pulled in part of her sweatshirt so that the fabric was balled in her grasp.

"I'm sorry that you had to see that..." I couldn't finish describing what we saw.

She wrapped her arms around her knees.

"I still see that when I close my eyes," she responded.

"I really had no intention of you witnessing anything bad like that, you have to believe me, Lauren. I just wanted to…" I sighed. "I didn't want you to get in the middle of the fight. I thought Ed could take care of himself and… and I don't know."

She finally turned to me a little but her eyes never left the spot she had been staring at.

"I didn't want you to get hurt. I saw them go into the house with the guns and I freaked."

"I'm sorry," she whispered again, closing

her eyes.

"What are you sorry for?" I questioned as my eyebrows scrunched together.

She had completely lost me now. I was confused on what she could possibly be sorry for.

"I watched Ed get shot and it was like the night the asteroids hit all over again. Here was someone willing to take us in and he was killed. Just after losing almost everyone. I'm afraid to see who's next. I didn't mean to blame you. You didn't put the gun to Ed's head."

Her voice was cracking like she was about to cry. Slowly, I reached out and pulled her chin gently toward me so that I could stare into her blue eyes. Her irises shined in the dark from the tears that were waiting to fall.

"It's alright," I spoke warmly.

"No it's not! I'm more worried now than ever! Look at what happened today—"

"I'm here to help you. You don't have to take on the weight of the world by yourself, Lauren," I said, slightly shaking my head., I was still holding onto her chin, and she made no attempt to pull away from me.

"We can't possibly protect ourselves from everything."

"We'll take it one step at a time."

She pulled her face away from me and gazed out into the distance.

"While we're in the talking mode, can I ask you something?" she asked before she bit down on her bottom lip.

"Sure, go ahead."

"Why did you kiss me?"

My eyes widened. That was definitely not the question that I was excepting from her.

"I really don't know, to tell you the truth," I answered, voice wavering.

There was silence between us. I peeked at her, and for the first time, I didn't know how to act around a girl. I hadn't been like this since the middle school. Being around her made me feel like that kid who didn't even know how to talk to girls. Since then, I've had a fair number of girlfriends, gotten my ear pierced, a tattoo, and learned to drive a motorcycle illegally. Bet when I was near Lauren, I couldn't even think of what to do. There were the times I was so overly protective I made a fool out of myself. She turned me into a puddle of mind-numbing mess.

"I'm going to sleep now. So night," she spoke, ending the humiliation for me of trying to find an answer.

She slid her body down and used her arm as a pillow with her back to me.

"Lake! Please, oh please, Lauren, let's go swimming!"

Sean was to the point of whining as he tried to get Lauren to ally with him and go swimming on this somewhat warm fall day. He let his eyes grow big as he tried the puppy face on his sister.

"You can't swim!"

I had let out a snort of laughter at this. Lauren turned to glare at me. She really knew how to narrow those eyes of hers.

"Come on, Lauren, please!" Paige begged as she joined forces with Sean.

They were quite a tag team.

"We don't know what's in the water." Lauren reasoned.

"I can tell you what's in the water," I nearly chuckled.

I whipped off my shirt as I ran out toward the water and threw my pants to the side. I attempted to not to trip as I jumped out of the leg holes. I made sure I created the biggest splash as I could as I hopped into the water.

When I came up for air, I had a grin on my face as the two were jumping up and down pleading even more to join me.

"I'm in the water! That's what!"

"You're a bad influence," she muttered as she rolled her eyes.

"Hey, I'm no Prince Charming." I laughed. "They never get to have any fun!"

I swam closer to her so I could splash her. She squeaked as the water hit her.

"What was that for?"

"Come in."

"You're not helping."

"You have to have fun every once in a while."

She put a foot in the water.

"It's freezing!" She squealed, withdrawing her foot out of the water the second her toes touched the water.

"You're such a girl."

"If you haven't noticed, I am a girl."

She placed her hands on her hips as she debated whether to go in or not. I saw the flicker of challenge in her eyes. I was more than aware of the fact that Lauren was a girl. There wasn't a moment that I could forget that.

"I'm not wearing a bathing suit," she

added, grasping for excuses.

"And that's a problem?" I asked with a smirk.

"There are kids here, you pervert!" yelled a fuming Cole.

"Put my shirt on then if you don't want yours wet."

"They can't swim," she added another justification.

"We can stay in the shallow part or have them on our backs. Come on, just come in and swim!"

She rolled her eyes as she thought.

"Hold on a second."

She grabbed my black sleeveless shirt then went behind a tree. Shortly afterward Lauren came out with the shirt ending a little above mid-thigh. I walked out of the water and grabbed Sean's hand as he was already in his bathing suit. Holding both of his hands, I swung him around, so his feet were in the water and he giggled.

"Me next!" Paige shrieked, excitedly jumping in the ankle-deep water.

I helped Sean climb on my back, so his arms were around my neck. I held out my hands for Paige who hopped up and took a hold of mine. Her hands disappeared in mine. I swung her around a little then put both down. I was a human jungle gym.

"Why aren't you guys coming in?" I eyed the rest of the group still standing on the bank.

Lauren rolled her eyes, then jumped into the water. She swam over to where we were, but she made sure that she kept the water at her shoulders in a poor attempt to hide herself from me.

Jill took off her shirt and pants just to show off that the two little ones weren't the only ones with bathing suits.

"Was I the only one who didn't think of going swimming at the party?" Lauren shrieked.

"Yup." Jill smiled as she did a cannon ball, which caused us to laugh.

Lauren put her arms over her head as a poor attempt of a shield.

"Aaron what's that on your back?"

Paige started to poke the tattoo. I could feel her fingers tracing the black ink as her other arm still clung around my neck.

"Um, that's a tattoo."

"Cool!" Sean spoke with excitement seeping through.

He jumped behind me to get a glimpse.

Lauren raised an eyebrow at me as I kept my back from her. I loved my tattoo, and it took up a good portion of my right shoulder blade. I didn't want to show her because she'd ask what it meant, and I still have absolutely no idea. I just thought that the design seemed cool, so I got it done. My dad took me to get it. He said he'd prefer that instead of me going with my friends and risk using an artist who used dirty needles and stuff. I didn't care as long as I got the tattoo. My dad said it would be our secret. Mom never found out. She would've buried us both in the backyard if she ever knew.

The ink was black and shaped like a sideways wave leading up to a swirl. The whirl had waves connected to it that led away from the main part of the design. At the top, there were two wavy lines going up with three ends facing right and three ending left. There were bat-like wings on each side of the stem. My tattoo was odd, but rather interesting, and unlike anything I had ever seen before.

Lauren started to swim around the water, pretending I wasn't there, which made me wonder if she could see the tattoo as she swam around. She just kept her eyes on Paige and Sean the entire time who were still climbing on me, then quickly glanced to make sure Mandy was alright with the other two. Finally, we took a day off from reality and had fun in the water like normal kids.

When the sky started to get darker, I decided that it was time to get out of the water. "It's time to get out, I think. So, we have time to dry off before it's completely dark. The nights are on the colder side now."

The two little ones started to whine, but we were stronger than they were and could lift them out. Everyone came out of the water, and when the air hit them, they began to shiver. We found pieces of wood from fallen trees. I put them in a pile and took out the glossy, black lighter from the pocket of my jeans. I set the wood near some rocks, then lit a fire, leaves quickly turning into ash; I wondered how much lighter fluid I had left in it. They all leaned near the flames as Lauren kept them from walking too close.

I watched the blaze dance on Lauren's face, and I stopped myself from getting closer to her. I grabbed my jeans and tugged them on when my boxers were dry from the swim. I sat down near the fire as the others slowly changed into their regular clothes. Lauren was the last to arrive, since she was helping the younger two like an overprotective mother even if it was clear they didn't need the aid. Then she, herself went to go change, leaving the little ones with us. When she came back, she threw my shirt back at me then sat not far from me as the two little ones behind us started to fall asleep.

Lauren held her hands out near the fire to warm them as she laughed at something Jill said, her fingers wiggled.

"You want to know what?" asked Jill.

"What?" Lauren asked.

"I guess I didn't need to do the summer reading then freak out about it. I didn't need to waste my time with all those stupid notes!"

Lauren gave a weak smile. "I guess I didn't need to spend my summer looking at colleges." Lauren eyes seemed to be glued to the flames now.

"I didn't even bother starting either." I chuckled.

Lauren just shook her head. My insides jumped as a small smile formed on her pink lips that glowed with the moving lights. Right then and there, I made a pact with myself. I couldn't let myself get close to her. I wasn't going to let myself fall in love with the odd girl from school.

She really wasn't out of the ordinary. She was nice, caring and just about everything that was different from the majority of school (which were the fashion and society worshipers). Lauren didn't care what others said about her because she liked herself the way she was.

I turned to look at Lauren one last time for the night as the flames died down. Her blue eyes locked with mine. The goal was to survive—not to fall in love. There was a silence in the air minus the slight crackling of the fire. With a saddened heart I knew I had to push her away in order for us to survive.

I woke up to find Lauren wasn't in the campsite. Everyone was sound asleep in our tight little section. I scanned the area and didn't see her, so I got up and searched the area. I found her sitting by the lake we swam in yesterday. She traced small patterns on the surface as I watched her for a couple of moments.

"We're going," I told her quietly so my words wouldn't sound like a command.

When we started out, we began to hear shouts and loud noises. Hesitantly, we went over to see what the racket was only to come upon what was left of a city. Some buildings had holes and parts were half missing. People were racing around, acting as if they could die at any minute. There were people punching each other in front of broken windows. Some people were making out in the alleyways. While others were so drunk, they were falling over, leaving others to walk over their lifeless forms.

The group turned to glance at me with pure shock in their eyes. The two little ones were trying to figure out what the people were doing. Lauren kept them close to her, and Jill covered their ears as curses were shouted into the air.

"There are people!" exclaimed Mandy.

There were people, about a hundred people. They didn't look too safe to be around as they were nearly killing each other, but there were people. The seven sins seemed to be hard at work here.

"We're not staying here," Lauren's expression was stern and serious as she growled this at me.

"Why not?"

"Are you even looking at that?" yelled Jill pointing at the crowd.

"We find a room and barricade ourselves

in there. We'll be fine."

"Are you nuts?" snapped Cole.

Apparently, they were taking turns to raise their voices at me.

"We need a break to get back our strength. We'll get some food. I know we're low."

"This place isn't safe! We could get robbed!" Lauren stressed.

"We could be raped!" screamed Jill.

Lauren gave a slight shudder.

"We're going there."

"No, we are not!"

Lauren was going to fight me on this one.

"No. We are going. Or else."

"Or else what?"

Lauren got me there. What could I possibly do to her? Well, what could I do to Lauren without breaking my pact with myself? I picked up Paige and headed down to the town as Lauren held Sean to her chest and the others began to form a tight cluster. Lauren kept yelling behind me to stop, but I wouldn't. We ran into one of the buildings that might have been an apartment or hotel at one point. There were some people on the floor passed out and some were yelling at others across the halls. I grabbed

Lauren's arm as I dragged them up the stairs until I found an empty room. I pushed them all in and locked the door behind us to the best I could.

"You've got to be kidding me," Lauren said. She was beyond angry.

There was a mattress in the middle of the room, but everything else seemed to be stolen. The bathroom door was hanging on a hinge. There were two windows in the one room of the place we got. One was broken while the other appeared to be stuck open. What did windows matter when you were on the fourth floor, right? It wasn't like someone could get in that way up here.

"Aaron, you and I need to talk," she said through gritted teeth.

Apparently, I wasn't the only one who was putting efforts into the notion to change their personality. It was obvious by the way she kept challenging me. Lauren dragged me into the bathroom and closed the door the best she could behind us.

"Hey, if you wanted me in the shower with you, all you had to do was ask."

What's wrong with a joke to lighten the air?

"Just shut up. You've been acting weird today, what's up?" she asked, poking my chest with a finger.

"Nothing's wrong."

She wasn't dumb.

"We need to take some time off from wandering. At least we know other people are alive."

"Yeah, we found people alive, the morally corrupt!"

She crossed her arms over her chest while standing in front of the door. I did not have to deal with this argument if I didn't want too. She should have been thrilled that I was even helping her.

"At least I found a place to stay."

"We were fine out there!"

"We needed to get off Manson's radar."

"We were in the woods!"

"He won't expect us to be here. He doesn't know about all of us. We don't need to be fighting about this. This is for the well-being of the group."

"The well-being of the group, are you nuts?" Her whole body was tensed as she shook her head furiously.

"Just because you don't like it here

doesn't mean it's not right."

"It's called your conscience Aaron." She nearly bit my head off as she spoke. "That tells you when something is not right. Ever heard of it?"

She raised an eyebrow at me.

"Look you'll have a roof over your head."

"We're not safe here! The door barely closes, the windows are broken—"

"We're too high for anyone to get in through the windows. There aren't even trees near the windows."

"That doesn't explain the door!"

"We're staying here. If you don't like it, too bad." I growled as I towered over her.

She turned her glance—I won. I gave a small smirk for my victory, knowing I still had power over her. I knew it was horrible to say, but I couldn't help but grin.

I walked out of the bathroom and grabbed the one chair that was in the main room to prop the wooden object against the door under the knob. I turned and moved my arms out to show her how I had fixed the door problem. Lauren just walked past me and stared out of the window. She wrapped her arms around herself. Summer was long gone as

November was probably just about to start. I couldn't believe it had been almost two months since that Labor Day weekend, which had ended so badly. I tried to keep track of the days, though it was getting harder.

A little while later, we ate the last of the food and went to sleep. I figured I would find some food tomorrow. We all squished together on that full mattress very tightly to the point we had to sleep on our sides so we could all fit. Lauren was at one end while I was on the other with everyone else smashed into the middle. We laid like that for two reasons, one so we knew everyone was fine and not going to leave. The second reason, well, she was still very pissed off at me. If I slept next to her, I'd have to sleep with one eye open.

I woke up to my stomach growling. I realized I was the only one awake. I stood up and stretched before I woke Lauren up. I rubbed her arm until she stirred. She didn't even open her eyes.

"What?" she asked bitterly, knowing it was me.

"I'm going to see if I can find food so

prop the chair against the door after me."

Lauren slowly got up and followed me to the door. It didn't take her long to shut me out in the hall. I ducked, dodge, and ran, attempting to avoid getting hit with random objects that were getting thrown across the building and outside. I finally managed to get into a building that had a slanted, half-blinking grocery store sign. The shelves were mostly bare so I took the few things that I could find as I heard a few gun shots. Running as fast I could, I jumped over pieces of what used to be buildings and ran back up the stairs.

"Lauren, let me in!" I yelled as I kicked the bottom of the door which bounced as I did so.

"How do I know it's you?"

I wanted to strangle her for leaving me in the hallway out of spite, as a plate whooshed past my ear to smash into a million pieces. I tried to think really hard of something that would bother her so she would know it was me.

"You have a birthmark on your upper thigh the size of a quarter," I smirked as I could see her red embarrassed yet livid face as she heard that.

I remembered seeing that when we were

swimming. I loved making that girl squirm with discomfort. She opened the door with her cheeks crimson just like I knew they would be and I smiled as I waltzed into the room. I dropped the stuff on the floor, kind of curious as to what I had even grabbed. It was mostly cereal so that was good, since for one, cereal didn't go bad as quickly if not opened and two, they ate it.

I collapsed onto the mattress that everyone moved from and tried to gain my breath back from my adventure. There was no way in hell I was going to tell Lauren that she was right about this place not being a good idea. I leaned my head back and closed my eyes, ready to go back to sleep.

"How do you know about the birthmark?" Lauren's voice was on edge.

I smiled big as I left my eyes closed for a second. I opened them just enough to see her feet and my grin widened as a thought came to me. She was going to want to kill me even more, but when I was talking about that birthmark of hers, I had to do this. I swiped my foot against her ankles which caused her to lose her balance and to fall onto the mattress. Acting swiftly, I straddled her waist and pined her wrists to the mattress. I stared into her wide, shocked blue eyes as I could see my chain hanging a couple of inches from my neck.

Every fiber in my body screamed at this action. My whole body shouted to kiss her. My mind blared at me that I was going against my goal to stay away from her. Yet at the moment, she tested me. I couldn't help but do it to her. The moment I had the chance to make her squirm my body commanded me to take the opportunity.

"The birthmark, I saw a little bit of it when we were swimming because my black shirt that you were wearing moved a lot. I didn't really know if it was there, but you just confirmed it."

The fear washed away from Lauren's jean blue eyes. Pure confusion settled in her eyes as she tried to figure out what I had planned to do. I was trying to figure out the real reason I had just pinned Lauren to the mattress.

"You cheated! You cheated; you jerk!" I heard Jill howled in the bathroom and I looked back down at Lauren very baffled.

"They found a deck of cards in the corner so they decided to play in the bathroom. I didn't want to ask questions."

My heart started to race. I forgot that

there were kids here with us that could be watching. Sean could have walked in to see me over his sister. I couldn't believe I was this close to her when I had my plan to work on. Then there was that biggest question that would beat all the questions. What the hell drove me to do this?

I quickly got off her and she got back up to go check on the card players, not looking back at me. I fell backward and groaned at how stupid I was acting, as my hands drove into my hair in frustration. I needed to get away from this. Well not this, but rather Lauren and the two little ones as they stared up at me so trusting and I was falling into this life too easily — the 'we're a family' formula. I stood up and went toward the door. I never felt so ashamed of myself, even more so than that day when I got Manson arrested, but I needed this to happen.

"Lauren, I'm leaving. I won't be back for a while," I called out my voice had no trail of emotion as my hand hovered over the handle of the door.

I knew something good could happen between us if we worked together — maybe a nice, long-lasting relationship could form. That could also lead to the group being stronger, well except for Cole plotting my death while I slept. I also knew she might have some not-so-nice words to say to me after what I had just done. If not words of anger at least more questions that I didn't have the answers to. So, I ran out before she could do anything. I needed to clear my head. I needed to figure a few things out. I was useless to them in this state. Even though half of me hated myself for doing this, but I knew I had to. I took off in the chaos, never looking back.

Roughly 100 days later...

7
Lauren

I curled up into a tighter ball in an attempt to keep warm. I didn't know what day it was, but I knew it was still on the brink of winter or at least that's what the temperatures made it feel like. The cold air blew through the broken glass and it caused our breath to show. Everyone else was still asleep in the warm clothes that I took from that house in Pennsylvania. They weren't warm enough, but they were better than the summer clothes we were in. My body felt numb as we tried to huddle together in a poor effort to keep warm. I had really taken heating for granted before this winter. I stared out the window while lying on the bed, not really believing the amount of snow on the trees in the distance or on the rooftops that could be seen from our room.

The town was quiet for once. It seemed everyone was asleep. At some point, everyone needed to rest. Suddenly, someone began to bang on the door. So, I had been wrong. I ran to the door and used all my weight to keep the person from coming in. I tried to muster up all the strength I could as I pushed my shoulder against the door.

"Go away!" I barked as a low groan escaped me from the struggle.

I pressed harder against the door when my feet started to slip against the title floor. I heard the person mumble as they fiddled with the doorknob. I gave one last push and shoved the chair under the knob after I heard the click. I still didn't trust the door and I leaned all my mass against it. I could still feel whoever was on the other side trying to get the door open. The person was not ready to give up for this apartment.

"Are they starting that already?" asked Cole, his voice groggy.

Cole stood up rubbing his head. His hair was getting long and grew out in every which way. Cole was not the only one who had lost weight from the long walks before we came here and smaller amounts of food we've had. I could see the results of weight loss on the others and I was afraid to even see if I looked the same way. Thankfully, there was no mirror. The others hadn't yet developed the hollow faces associated with malnourishment. I wouldn't let it get to that.

"Yeah and it's amazing they haven't given up yet," I grumbled still against the door, not really feeling it budging more.

"At least we can protect ourselves."

I let out a sigh as I let my head fall back against the now still door.

"For how much longer though?" I sighed, my eyes glued to the ceiling, unable to meet Cole's. His voice was stronger than I felt.

"You and I have been doing great with protecting them," Cole responded in a tender tone, while he walked over to me.

When Cole reached me, he wrapped an arm around my shoulders, bringing me into his chest. I rested my face against the nape of his neck, feeling the world draining all of my energy and hope from every fiber of my body. Cole's other hand slowly, almost clumsily, caressed up and down my back. His head lowered so that his cheek was against my forehead. I slipped out of his arms, turning my back to him, so that I wouldn't be able to see his reaction. Not sure if I had the heart or energy to see his expression.

"We can't stay here too much longer," I whispered, feeling so unlike my old self as I stared at the ceiling. I prayed that the awkwardness would pass.

"Are you willing to leave without Aaron?" Cole whispered in a tone I couldn't read. He didn't move from his spot by the door even though my back still to him.

I really didn't want too, but Aaron was leaving us no choice.

"We should at least wait until winter is done," I spoke in a low voice, ready to move on.

"Are you being smart with that choice or do you still think he'll come back? Just like the last time you made us wait."

I still stared at the cracking ceiling above us. My heart started to beat faster as I tried to figure out what the true answer to that question. I really had no response since I didn't know the answer myself. How can I choose to go out into the cold and possibly abandon one of us or stay here to wait while supplies were dangerously low? Both situations were hazardously awful.

"It's the best for us not to be out in this

weather," I partially lied.

Another week went by as we hid in that
room, bored out of our minds. It seemed cabin
fever had taken over. Sean and Paige were
getting antsy, not able to stay much longer in a
small area. Not being allowed to leave, stuck
with just us in addition to the two stuffed
animals, they were anxious. I knew we would
have to leave soon. I started to pack up what we
had left of the food, since we would be leaving
that day. I'd finally decided this place wasn't
safe and food in the town was running out. We
came here when conditions were bad. I couldn't
believe that the area found a way to become
worse.

As I was getting the bag ready, there was
a pounding on the door, loud hammering that
shook the doorknob. My heartbeat raced as I ran
to the door to keep it closed.

"Let me in, girl!"

I tried even harder to keep the door
closed as I realized the person knew I was a girl.
Jill took Sean and Paige into the bathroom.

"Go away!" I yelled, but I could hear the
strain in my voice.

This guy was stronger than the other person.

"Lauren! Open the damn door now!" The voice growled.

I nearly jumped when I heard that. That voice sounded familiar, but when was the last time I heard it? Why did he know my name? Was that who I thought it was?

"Lauren, open the damn door now. I'm hurt! Open the damn door!"

Moving fast, my fingers fumbled as I moved the chair and opened the door. As the door swung open, I pulled Aaron into the room and put the chair back. He fell onto the mattress in the middle of the room and I looked at him, barely recognizing the guy before me. Aaron was covered in dirt and his skin was red from the cold. He had barely noticeable blond stubble on his face, but what got to me was the cloth wrapped around his left bicep. I fell by his side.

"What happened?" I shrieked.

Aaron closed his eyes as he held his left arm out to the side. My hands shook as they traveled near the cloth.

"Aaron, you're back!" sang Paige blissfully. She clapped her hands together as she beamed.

I looked and my face grew pale, trying to figure out what had happened Aaron.

"Paige, how about you go pick up the cards with the others in the bathroom so that we can put them in my bag for later."

Paige skipped out without a word. I leaned close to his face and I pushed away the stray hair from his eyes.

"What happened?"

Aaron finally opened his eyes. My heart skipped a beat at seeing those eyes. His eyes made my knees wobbly, and I thanked God I was already on the ground. Never had those blue orbs hit me like this. They weren't their normal bright, blue eyes that were cool and semi-tyrannical with a smartass way about them. Now they had a worn out and wounded appearance to them.

"Manson's men caught up with me at one point. The bullet just skimmed my arm. It got cold!" he spoke softly into my ear as I leaned nearer so the younger ones wouldn't hear.

"When did this happen?"

He closed eyes again. I started to worry even more.

"Aaron!" I nearly shouted as I shook his non-injured shoulder.

"I'm fine, just tired," Aaron mumbled.

"You're not fine! You were shot!" I stammered; my voice sounded stressed as alarm set in.

"I'll be fine," Aaron spoke in an even voice with a shrug of a shoulder.

"We'll leave when you recuperate."

"No we'll go soon."

"No! I have just as much power here as you do! You're injured, so I make up the rules," I said, taking charge.

Aaron has been gone all this time and he thought he was in charge? I'd been the one taking care of everyone. I protected everyone. I was the one in charge. I had to learn to be tough and he was going to have to deal with it. He just gazed into my eyes. I watched the calculations forming in his head, to argue that point or not with me.

I started to untie the cloth as he attempted to move his arm away. I unsecured the cloth before he could do anything. As my hands grazed his skin, the flesh was cold as ice. My mouth dropped when I saw the small cut. The cut was four inches long, red and swollen with some dried blood around it. I wondered if he really took care of the cut when he was gone. If I had money, my bet would be on no.

"Aaron—"

"It just needs to be cleaned and I need to sleep for at least a night, then we'll go." His head fell so he could peek at his injury.

I glanced into his eyes and realized he really needed to get some rest. Underneath his eyes was so dark, a rich purple color painted against his light skin.

"Jill," I called. "Bring everyone in here and give them something to eat."

I helped Aaron up then brought him into the bathroom as everyone else went over to the food by the mattress. I looked around for something to clean his cut with but couldn't find anything. The amount toilet paper we had left was running low, I turned toward the sink as spurts of water sprayed out harshly. The water pipes connected to the water plant must have been low as obviously no one worked there anymore. The pipes must be mostly frozen as well. I assisted Aaron as I put his arm under the water, and we cleaned the cut the best we could. Neither of us said a word, but I could feel his eyes on me the whole time.

"It's rude to stare," I finally said, using my fingers to clean the cut before dabbing the sensitive skin with some of his shirt.

"You have no idea how afraid I was that you guys moved on," Aaron answered.

My heart raced rapidly at the sound of his deep voice as I tried to avoid his eyes. Instead, I looked at his cut.

"That was what we were going to do today actually. You have impeccable timing yet again," I continued in hushed tones.

That time I had welcomed Aaron back home open arms.

"You all are alive and not sick, right?" he asked, and I could still feel his gaze.

I looked at the cloth again as I tied it in a nice knot to keep the fabric in place without hurting him. I don't think I could hurt him. Although it seemed he lost weight, he still had his lean muscles. He had to be too cold to really feel anything anyway. Yet he seemed small from the weight loss.

"We're all fine," I spoke as an attempt to reassure him.

"That's good. I didn't have any intention of staying away that long." He sounded sincere and a little lost.

"I don't even know why you left in the first place," I answered, finally catching his eyes for a mere second.

There was a quiet pause as I stood up shunning his eyes from mine.

"I had to leave," he said, each word seemed almost like its own sentence.

"Why?"

"I can't explain it." Aaron took a moment taking a deep breath. "Lauren, just trust me when I say I had too."

I sighed, not believing how secretive he had been with us. The secrets were bothering me and that he wanted to be that way. I looked at him finally realizing he was shaking a little.

"How did you survive in the cold like this?" I asked, my hands hovering over his shoulders. I refrained from rubbing them.

We walked into the other room to find everyone finishing up what they were eating.

"I have no idea."

He sat down on the mattress then took a small handful of cereal. He lay down after he ate. The others were quietly watching his movements. Each face had a different expression. No one knew what to say. I glimpsed down at Sean and he took a step forward. I quickly grabbed Sean as he tried to jump on top of Aaron.

"Aaron, you're back!"

"Hey there, little buddy. Have you been taking good care of your sister?" Aaron asked affectionately as he ruffled Sean's hair.

"Yeah, I took real good care of her." Sean answered with a giggle.

I smiled as I let Sean go which turned out to be a mistake. Sean jumped onto Aaron, laughing, and sat on Aaron's chest.

"Sean, get off him!" I yelped as I leaned over and grabbed Sean.

"Lauren, I'm fine!"

Okay, so now we were both being stubborn. This shall be interesting.

"Let's just get some sleep so we can leave early tomorrow," Aaron said, keeping his gaze on mine.

"Great, we're getting orders from him again." Cole groaned with a roll of his eyes.

I ended up next to Aaron when we all lay down to sleep. I squished myself as close as I could to him so I could be on the mattress. While Aaron had been gone, we had a little more room on the bed.

I could feel his icy skin through my clothes. A shiver went through me and I couldn't believe someone could be alive and feel that frozen. I sat up and took off my sweatshirt, then placed the material on him like a blanket. I curled up close to him so that I wouldn't freeze. I buried my face into the nap of his neck, trying to keep warm and not fall off the bed. Slowly, I closed my eyes, and I felt an arm wrap around me. Aaron pulled me in tightly.

It snowed so much the next day we were blocked in the room for another week. Sean and Paige were going crazy in the close quarters. I tried to search for more food and could only find a few packages of raisins. I knew raisins wouldn't be enough for all of us, but the shrunken grapes were better than nothing. On the way back, one of the rooms was left wide open as the people ran out, taking their chance with the storm that dwelled on the outside. They were running for dear life toward what might very well be their deaths. There, lying on the floor of the room was a large black leather jacket. I took the object and ran up into our room.

"Aaron, look what I found," I said as I placed the chair in front of the door.

Aaron turned to look at me and caught the jacket I tossed at him. he tugged on the jacket and rubbed his arms as he gave me a smirk, his eyes gleaming. The black leather fit him well. The coat was baggy, but not huge.

"Thanks."

"Hey, no problem. We can't have you freeze and die on us. We might actually need you," I teased. I smiled and gave a small laugh.

"You think that's funny, don't you?"

"Of course, I do."

Aaron stood over me, a little cleaner than he was when I left. I stared into his eyes as I continued to smile. Aaron's dark cobalt eyes smirked down at me and I wondered what he really had been up to all those months while I had to deal with all questions from the kids. Why aren't we in school right now? Is Santa going to be able to find us? Where are our parents?

Sean and Paige couldn't stop asking me things. I hadn't fully told them what had happened to the world. I just told them that our lives were very different and harder now; that discussion hadn't gone over too well.

As I gazed at him, it made me kind of forget the hardship we had to deal with since he left. During those months I realized I had to be tough, that I had to change how I was. I had to be stronger than before. I had to work harder on not falling for Aaron so easily, especially if he was going to keep disappearing on us.

"Why wouldn't I think that is funny?" I asked, tilting my head so that I could see his eyes better.

"Because first of all, I was freezing my butt off, but you curling up to me at night did make up for that—"

"Well that's done with," I added cutting him off, his eyes hazy, smirk full on shinning.

"But it's so cold and I don't know how you guys survived this long in the cold." Aaron became serious.

"Not well, it was hard and bitter, but we are here, standing in front of you."

I looked over to the group playing cards in the corners as they were pulling their sweatshirts closer to them. I really wanted to get out of here since food was at an all-time low in the area, but we couldn't move on with the weather and I was really worried now. It seemed like all our problems before this seemed stupid, but our chances of survival were looking awfully by the second.

"It's a good thing that you guys did," Aaron answered softly, the muscles in his shoulders stiffened, his hands were restless by his sides.

"Yeah it is," I answered keeping my eyes on the group even through their chattering teeth I could hear their giggles or arguments over the rules of their game; an attempt to keep things normal.

I stood there with Aaron watching the others as I felt his fingers reach out toward mine as kind-heartedly as butterfly wings before interlacing with mine. Our hands locked.

We were there for another two weeks as the snow gradually melted away. The food was gone, and I listened as the smaller children cried out for food. It was heart wrenching when I couldn't do anything for them. So, we headed out of the rotten town and I for one couldn't have been any happier to see the town getting smaller as we walked away from that hell pit.

I held Sean close to me as Jill had Paige on her back. Sean's fingers were curled into his sweatshirt, his face in mine as he tried to keep warm. I could hear Sean's light snoring as we got farther and farther away from the city. They were all now too tried from lack of food to really go far.

"Aaron, we seriously need to find more food now, because if I have to listen to them cry like I had for the past two weeks, I'll go insane from heartbreak." Sean whimpered and I brought him in closer. I nuzzled the top of his head through his hood.

Aaron sighed, not even trying to look at me.

"I don't know how well we'll do in finding something to eat, but we'll try."

Not the response I was looking for, which made me aggravated, but there was no other answer he could really give while being truthful. So, we traveled awhile longer until we came to a house which was slanted, faint smoke climbing out of the chimney stack. The home looked like it wasn't doing well, but the smoke showed someone actually currently lived there. Signs of life.

"You think it'll be worth checking it out?" I asked.

I glanced at Aaron. He appeared deep in thought as he looked at the house.

"It could be another Ed," I whispered.

"If so, me getting harassed by another old guy is not what I am looking for."

I rolled my eyes. "Suck it up. Let's go see who lives in the house there."

I trudged ahead of them and knocked lightly on the door; afraid the wood would fall down if I hit it too hard. I heard the thuds of footsteps and I now regretted knocking on the door. When the door opened, I couldn't believe what stood before me. A tall, dark-haired woman with strong limbs stood there, but the part I hadn't been expecting was that the woman was pregnant. I found myself gapping at the woman in the doorway, unable to find the words to greet her.

"What do you want?" she questioned bitterly, a hand behind her on her lower back, and the other on her rounded stomach.

"Yeah, we were wondering if you could spare some shelter or food—" Aaron started to only be interrupted.

"I bet you would. You males are out to use us. Then when you get what you want, you leave. You males love to use females."

I nearly laughed. I'm going to guess a guy got her pregnant and left. Yet I didn't chuckle, knowing this was one of my fears in life too, which might be a common fear among girls. Though I also wanted to laugh at the fact that we found another person, and Aaron had become their verbal punching bag.

"Please, if you could at least spare a little amount of food for the two little ones, we'll be out of your hair as soon as you want us to be," I piped in, as Sean yawned on cue peeking at the woman.

She glimpsed at Sean and Paige, then sighed in annoyance. She walked aside so we could enter the home, which was missing furniture. Well there were a couple of pieces, but nothing homey, the home was one big room with a bed with a few thin sheets, and a small kitchen on the side. In the fireplace though were wooden pieces, I was not sure though if I saw fabric burning in the mists of flames.

"Thank you so much."

The others curled onto the couch. The lady kept glancing between Aaron and me, as I placed Paige and Sean at the table.

"There is a little bit of food in the cabinet right there."

I opened the cabinet and took out some food, then placed it in front of them. I gave them some but made sure not to seem overbearing on this generous person. Slowly, they woke up and ate. I felt relief wash over me at the sight of them eating.

"Are they yours?" Her sour voice came out bluntly.

"Excuse me?" I asked, completely confused.

"Are they your kids?"

My eyes widened and Aaron let out a short snort of laughter.

"That's my brother and his friend!" I responded, my voice hitting high octaves.

"That's the second time someone thought Sean was your kid." Aaron let out another short laugh his grin was wide as he restrained himself.

"Who was the other?" I asked feeling insulted that someone thought I looked like I had a kid, let alone a six-year-old.

"Ed..."

"Why does everyone think I have kids?"

I was angry now. Did I look like someone who would have had kids at this age? Or did I physically look like I had kids? The answer to either of those questions had better be no.

"I don't know, but Ed thought I was the father," Aaron responded, shrugging his shoulders not looking at me anymore, his smirk long gone from his new comment.

All the talk of Ed made dread seep

through my body. The emotion dripped down from my head like fresh paint that dripped down a wall. Why would Ed think that Aaron and I were parents?

"Yeah, don't ever have sex or you could end up like me. I haven't seen the father in a while, and I don't think he's coming back. Men suck!" the woman growled; eyebrows fused.

"You do realize there are a few men here?" Aaron asked, glaring at the woman.

"I don't see men; I just see little boys who think they're men. Guys just don't grow up; they just grow taller and horny."

My jaw dropped. Was this woman serious? I could not believe my ears.

"Look, I get you're pissed at the baby's father, but don't insult me or them. Don't insult our gender like that. You don't know me or Cole or even little Sean here and I'll shut up now because I don't want to get into an argument with a pregnant woman."

They glowered at each other and I couldn't believe they were in a sexist argument after just meeting a minute ago. This wasn't looking good. Apparently, she was as stubborn as Aaron, so things didn't seem so good for us being able to stay there. Was it going to be hard for Aaron to cooperate with the few people we hopefully would come across?

"Look, you can stay here tonight just because of them little ones, but you're going to have to leave tomorrow first thing in the morning."

The woman turned tightly on her heel and went over to the bed to lie down. She looked like once she was down, she wasn't about to get up anytime soon because she was pretty much immobile. I turned to glance at Aaron, narrowing my eyes at him.

"What?" He tried to give me an innocent look.

I hit him upside the head. He started to glare at me.

"What was that for?" He rubbed the back of his head.

"Behave yourself!"

"She started it!" Aaron said, sounding like a five-year-old caught throwing sand.

I rolled my eyes. I had gained another child to take care of. The woman might be right about the not growing up thing.

"You're arguing with a pregnant woman who took us in. Repeat that in your head to hear how ridicules that sounds." I snapped as I pointed a finger in his face.

"You're defending someone who insults me and doesn't give us her name?"

"We didn't exactly give her our names either," I responded in muted manner.

"You're just helping her because you're both women."

I let out a sigh and rolled my eyes as I went to join the others.

"Girl—" snapped the woman.

"Girl has a name, and it's Lauren." I let my frustration and anger be heard in my voice as I answered the woman.

The woman stared at me blankly.

"I'm Jackie. So how did you end up with stick up the butt?" Jackie spoke, and I noticed her tone was naturally acidic.

I didn't have to ask who she had meant. I sat on the edge of the bed, gazing down at the sheets.

"That's Aaron. It's a long story," I answered truthfully, as I wondered when she would kick me off her bed.

She rolled her eyes. "He's a pain, isn't he?"

"You realize he is right there, right?" I questioned, pointing with my eyes.

I was shocked by her always sour attitude and her boldness. Maybe Jackie's character wasn't boldness, but rudeness.

"So, you're afraid of him?"

"No. Why should I be?" I jolted a little from shock, with a raised eyebrow.

"Good, don't be afraid of the males." The word males came out like it was the vilest word she had ever uttered.

"How about you get some sleep," I suggested, nor sure if she should be that fired up in her condition.

She let out a snorting laugh. "How old are you, girl?"

"Seventeen."

"So, you're not much younger than me, yet we have to act older to take care of others while the men don't do a thing."

"I do things!" Aaron shouted from the kitchen.

I wanted to laugh, but Jackie gave me a death stare. I bowed my head and bit my lip as heat rose to my cheeks.

"You all just go to sleep now," she growled.

We all fell asleep on the floor close together so we wouldn't bother the crazy woman anymore.

An excruciating scream pierced through the first peaceful night we've had. I bolted up and so did the others. I looked around, trying to figure out where that scream came from and when I found its origin, I could feel the blood drain from my body. My knees became weak. Jackie was on the bed looking like those women we saw in health movies right before they gave birth. I wanted to run out of the house at that moment as the nausea hit me.

"What the hell is going on?" Aaron asked with sleep still clouding his eyes.

"Aaron, I'll give you a hint, she's pregnant. What the hell do you think is wrong with her after being that pregnant?" I shrieked with my wide eyes locked onto Aaron's.

Realization overcame his face.

"Oh no, there's no way in hell I'm watching a woman give birth!"

"Shut up and help me!" Jackie bellowed.

My eyes widened to their limits.

"Jill, take the others in the other room. Aaron, you're staying with me. If I'm going down, I'm bringing you down with me."

"Are you nuts, I'm not doing that!" Aaron's voice nearly cracked.

"Too bad." I grabbed his arm and yanked him closer to me.

I pulled him up as Jackie let out another scream. I so didn't want to do this. Wasn't there a way we could leave her? No, we couldn't leave her at that moment. We had to help her. Damn conscience!

"You get the bottom, I'll get the screaming head," Aaron said, not looking well as he kept his eyes on the ground.

"Wait, why do you get the head?"

Jackie screamed again, even more infuriated. I jumped and I thought I saw Aaron do the same.

"Because you're to go through this sometime in the future."

"Shut the fuck up and help me!"

I don't know whose words were more powerful at that moment, but I pushed that aside as I walked disgusted toward the area that baby was going to come out. I really had no idea what to expect or anything since when it came to this part of the movie in health class, I wasn't paying attention. Jackie screamed again and I looked at Aaron because I really had no idea what to do!

"Lift up the dress, you moron!" Jackie screeched.

I followed her directions, instantly trying to get the images out of my head. Aaron gave the woman his hands to squeeze to get her mind off the pain. I saw him flinch when she did so. She pushed and before I knew it I had a slimy being in my arms that was crying out into the night. I took hold of one of the sheets that was tossed to the side and wrapped the baby in it after cutting the umbilical cord. I handed the baby over to her, not believing how small the child was. It is strange to think that we were all that size at one point. I remembered when Mom and Dad brought Sean home. He was cute.

I felt tired and happy as I watched Jackie hold the baby close to her. A calmer side of Jackie showed through as she held it. Her eyes became softer and didn't seem like they could move away from her own child. The muscles in Jackie's face relaxed. She brought up a finger and tenderly stroke the baby as it slowed the babe's tears. At that moment I started to wonder what gender the baby was.

"Jackie, is the baby a boy or a girl?"

She lifted the sheets a little, made a slight

face, then the baby grabbed onto her hand. The baby was so cute.

"It's a boy," she said affectionately cleaning the little boy up.

Aaron let out a laugh and Jackie glared at him.

"He's very cute," I stated before an argument brewed between the two.

"He is, isn't he?" She appeared so happy holding him. "Thank you very helping me, you two."

"You're welcome, but I need to go clean up —"

"The bathroom is right there. Feel free to take a quick shower if it works."

"Thank you."

I walked into the bathroom and locked the door behind me. I turned on the water and the sound was music to my ears. The water came out in spurts, but a shower was a shower. I quickly took off my clothes and noticed how gross they were now. As the water was warming up, I rinsed my clothing out quickly. The second the water was the slightest bit warm, I jumped in to take my shower. As I scrubbed my arms harshly to rid of the evidence, one thought ran through my mind, and only one thought.

My hands started to shake as the words echoed through my mind. My breath shortened and I sat on my feet in the shower now fearing the words. Many thoughts ran through my mind as I tried to figure out what Aaron meant with that one sentence.

"Because you're to go through this sometime in the future."

8
Aaron

Never in my entire life did I want to watch a woman go through birth. God! Where did women get that strength to almost break a male's hand out of nowhere? I couldn't believe Lauren dragged me into helping her. I mean, come on, childbirth was a girl thing unless it's your own child. Not only did she drag me into this chaos, but she also left me out here with this mess. There was no way I was cleaning that.

"You never told me your name."

I turned around to look at the woman just to spin back around. I so didn't want to watch a woman breastfeed. The act of breastfeeding a baby just made me uncomfortable and grossed me out. I walked in on my aunt breastfeeding my cousin when I was eight; that image never left me as much as I wanted it to.

"The name's Aaron."

"My name is Jackie. How about you knock on the door for Lauren to speed it up?"

I just nodded my head, unable to say another word. I could hear the shower water turn off. Two minutes later, Lauren came out with a fluffy bathrobe tied tightly around her. I knew she had lost a lot of weight over the last few months. Being sick at the beginning of our journey and not having real time to recover left her small and fragile that I had noticed the second I came back. All three times she was thinner than the time before.

"I hope you don't mind me borrowing—"

"Not at all. You washed your clothes, didn't you?" Jackie cut off Lauren.

"Yes—"

"Don't worry about it."

Lauren was wearing *just* a bathrobe then. Don't think that way, Aaron. You'll scare Lauren. Don't think that way right after what you just watched. Watching a live birth can act as the best form of birth control on a seventeen-year-old guy.

"Jackie, not to be rude, but I think we'll sleep in the other room to give you some space,"

Lauren said, her arms crossed firmly over the seam of the sides of the robe as her eyes were where the others were.

"Okay, whatever suits you." Jackie shrugged still watching the child in her arms.

Lauren walked into the room where the others were sat quietly. I wondered why she seemed like she wasn't really there. She was distant. Even when she seemed out of it, she was still driving my body crazy.

"Hey, Sean, guys, let's get some sleep."

She knelt and helped the others get tucked in under a blanket on the floor. I watched as she fiddled with robe to keep it closed and I wanted to laugh at her. Quickly, everyone got close in order to fall asleep while Cole kept quiet moving closer to where Lauren sat. He was nearer than he normally would be. Cole was silent as he smirked at me as if he won something. I glared at Cole as I kept an eye on him most of the night. There was something unsettling about him and I truly did not want him near Lauren, especially in her current wardrobe.

"Are you guys sure you have to go?"

Jackie was sitting on the bed with the sleeping child in her arms.

"Yes, I think we have to get on our way." I tried to hide my eagerness to get away from what seemed to be a bipolar woman and a newborn.

I was inching out of the door ahead of the others. I started to pull Lauren with me, but Lauren flinched. I let my hand fall from her arm, completely bewildered. I mean, she's never done that before. She didn't even meet me in the eyes as she started to head west like our plan. We weren't going out, not that I was sure that the rules of dating could really be applied now, but still Lauren never cared about the small touches on the hand before. I mean, when we were first starting on this expedition, Lauren was the one grabbing my hand.

"Bye, Jackie," the group spoke in unison over their shoulders.

Then we headed on our way with a small noise of a door closing. We kept walking in silence. I kept watching Lauren; she wasn't speaking to me, Mandy was shy, Cole hated me, and Jill was a peacemaker.

"Lauren?"

"Yes, Sean."

"Where did Jackie's baby come from?" Sean asked, holding Lauren's hand, his head titled up to see her face.

I wanted to laugh.

"Um...well the baby came from—"

"Her tummy," answered Paige as she held Lauren's other hand and peered around Lauren to look at Sean, "My aunt was pregnant last year, and the baby came from her tummy."

"Was that why Jackie was fat?" Sean asked innocently.

"She wasn't fat Sean she had a baby inside her," Lauren corrected.

"She still looked fat!"

"You shouldn't say that to a girl's face, or they'll pound you into the ground." I paused as I picked up Sean and put him on my back. He held his well-worn stuffed animal tight. "You know, with that added weight, they could sit on you and crush you."

He giggled.

"Nice thing to teach him, Aaron." Jill snapped at me for what felt like the first time.

"It was just a joke, Jill," I chuckled.

"Of course, since you guys can't have children, it's a joke."

"Wait, I can't have a baby? That's not fair

that girls can, and I can't." Sean pouted.

"Trust me, little buddy, you should be happy about that."

"Why?" Sean asked as he was close to my ear, curiosity was drenched in each letter.

"Yeah, why should he be happy about that?" Jill asked, using a tone that told me if I said the wrong thing, I was going to be killed.

I didn't know how to answer that one. When you're in a group of seven and only three of the people are guys, but only one of the guys likes you while the other wanted your head on a wall, I really didn't know how to answer that. I glanced over at Lauren for help, but she wasn't paying attention.

"Lauren, are you, all right?"

Changing the subject is a good way to not have to answer the question!

"Yeah I'm fine, just not talkative today."

The rest of the way was quiet as Jill was irritated with me. I couldn't figure out what was wrong with Lauren and her silence started to really get to me. Sean didn't want to talk because he was annoyed about not being able to have babies when girls could. Mandy was just always quiet anyway and I just didn't want to understand Cole.

We finally stopped as night approached as the temperature dropped even more. I started a fire as we sat around and ate some of the berries we found after what felt like an hour of arguing over if they would be poisonous or not. Paige and Sean were the first to fall asleep in our laps so we put them on the ground so they could sleep more soundly. Lauren then curled into a ball as she watched the flames in the middle us. I scooted a little closer to her. Before I knew it, we were listening to Cole's snores, knowing the rest were asleep. Lauren always seemed to have trouble falling asleep.

"Lauren, you want to tell me what's really wrong?"

"I'm fine, it's…" Lauren started, her voice drifted off leaving just stillness once more.

"It's what?"

She let out a quiet sigh. I so didn't want Lauren to be sick again. I don't think our group could handle that and I wasn't about to walk back to Jackie's for Lauren to get better. I had a feeling that I would have become Jackie's personal whipping boy if we went back.

"It's probably nothing." Lauren sighed again, her eyes never leaving the fire.

There was a snap of a branch, glancing in

the direction of the sound, I saw nothing.

"What was that?" Lauren looked nervous.

"How about you tell me what's going on with you, and I'll tell you there is nothing out there," I responded, glancing back at her.

She was probably just over thinking something. So, I wasn't going to expect a big problem. I watched her as she continued to stare at the blaze before us.

"What did you mean when you said, 'you're to go through this sometime in the future'?"

I raised an eyebrow at her. I said that when Jackie was about to give birth; that I do remember.

"That's what has been bothering you?" I asked, evenly.

That didn't sound like a big deal.

"Yes, now what did you mean by that?"

Lauren titled her head as she glanced at me with heartbreaking, befuddled, blue eyes. Then she turned back toward the flames, almost like she was unable to keep her gaze on mine.

"I thought that was pretty self-explanatory," I answered, not seeing her point.

What was wrong with what I said?

She turned to stare at me now, really

looked at me in the eyes so that I could see her racing emotions from within.

"Who said anything about me going to have children though?"

"Don't girls want to have children?" I inquired with a shrug.

"Not all of us." Lauren shrieked before her voice softened. "Well, maybe I did at one point, but I don't think I would want to bring children into this kind of world."

"The world has and never will be safe—"

"No, but at least before the children wouldn't have been starving." Her voice hitting a high pitch as she cut me off.

"You're saying you don't want to have children because you're afraid for their lives?" I asked in an even voice. "That's what parents do."

"Not like this, Aaron. We don't even know if more asteroids are coming to finish us off. Or if Manson is behind a tree right now, waiting to kill us in our sleep. I don't think I could go through that kind of labor we just helped Jackie with. Only to have that child die." Her voice was small and frightened.

"I understand that, but the world needs people again," I answered, trying to be sensitive to her stress level.

She wasn't making sense. I mean, what was she so worked up about?

"No, it doesn't. You're not going forced me into something I don't want to do." I watched her jaw muscles tighten in the dancing flames.

"What am I forcing you into?"

"Into having children, and who are you going to try to breed with me?" She was full out angry now. "You?"

"I'm not trying to breed you. Wait! What's wrong with me?"

What would be so wrong if Lauren and I had kids? Being patient and kind was no longer possible in this discussion. I tried, but that ship had sailed. I'd left to give us space because I thought we were getting too close, and I came back to realize I couldn't really just wish away feelings toward Lauren. I'd come to terms with feelings I had, only to have Lauren pretty much tell me she was this disgusted even thinking about having kids with me.

"Forcing someone to have sex for the outcome of children only, is called breeding. So, don't try to pretty it up."

I felt my blood boil.

"You didn't answer my question," I muttered between my teeth.

"And what was your question, you jerk?" Lauren growled through gritted teeth.

"What is wrong with me and you?" I asked, unable to hold back my tone.

"Us? Are you kidding me? First of all, we're seventeen years old!"

"It's not like we're in school anymore."

I stood up and she followed, both of us narrowed our eyes at each other. The distance between us was just enough for us to stab each other in the chest with our fingers.

"So, we should have children purely on the fact that the school is now a pile of rubble?"

"That's not what I meant."

"Then what did you mean?"

I wanted to shake her but knew I would never lay a hand on Lauren or any other girl.

"I just meant that we're adults now in this situation and we have to—"

"Have sex and bring children into a world full of disaster that'll make them wish they were dead?"

"Will you let me finish a sentence and stop cutting me off?" I snapped.

We tried to kill each other with our glares.

We were whispering argumentatively instead of yelling as we were trying not to bring the others into the dispute. My hands were in fists by my sides while her arms where crossed over her chest tightly. I could feel the fury vibes radiating off her and I bet I wasn't exactly sending calm vibrations either.

"If you weren't being so ridiculous, I wouldn't have to cut you off."

"I'm being ridiculous? I'm only talking about the future for us."

"It doesn't sound like you are talking far into the future."

"Well, pregnancy is unexpected."

"Only when you're currently having sex." Lauren pointed out.

I wasn't going to let her know that she was right. I wasn't going to let her win an argument even if I had no idea why we were arguing in the first place. It wasn't like I said I wanted to have kids now either. I just said the future. She read too much into my words, which now caused a riff.

"Why do you care all of a sudden about having children?" Lauren asked.

"I don't know. Having kids is just one of those things that people do."

I didn't know the answer to be honest. Sean and Paige grew on me?

"No, that's not why people have children. A couple has children because they actually have some form of emotions toward one another and—"

"Who says we don't have feelings for each other?" I shot back at Lauren.

I thought back about how her eyes locked with mine when I had pinned her to the mattress before I left. Lauren had not fought to get me off her, or any other time we touched each other in one form or another. Lauren had never argued or went against me with any of our other gestures before this.

"Well, how do you feel about me then?" Her tone softened as she gazed into my eyes. Her shoulders loosened.

Her eyes were not glowering balls of fury anymore, they were just a peaceful blue sky.

"I don't…" I said, hearing the tone drop in my own voice.

"Argh! You're so annoying!" She let out an irritated groan and stomped away from the group toward the wooded area.

"Where do you think you're going in the dark?" I wasn't sure if I was more panicked about what was out there or wound up from our heated words.

"I need to let off some steam," she yelled back not even turning to look at me.

"Not in the dark!"

"Watch as my back disappears!" Lauren nearly shouted with a wave over her head in my direction.

"Just come back here and go to sleep."

"I bet you would like me to go to sleep, you pervert." she snapped back, turning to glare at me quickly with her arms out wide.

I had the need to punch something as she walked into the shadows. I couldn't believe she was doing something that stupid. Fine, go. See what I care if something happens! She'll want to apologize tomorrow anyway. I lay back on the ground using my arm as a pillow. I glanced to see they all slept even through our quarrel. I fell asleep never to have felt or heard her come back.

9
Lauren

So easy for Aaron to talk about having children. He wouldn't be the one who would be carrying the baby for nine months before labor. I mean, come on. Who would want to bring a child into this kind life? We could barely take care of ourselves as it was, and he wanted to add more mouths. What a moron. Furthermore, if you're trying to talk someone into having your children, you should have some sort of feelings toward them. Or be able to tell them you love them.

I stomped through the woods, not caring about the amount of noise I made. I needed to blow off steam although wandering through the woods wouldn't have been my first choice. I knew Aaron was right. Wandering off alone at night was stupid, but there was no way I was going to listen to him or let him know that he was right. I wished I had watched more carefully at where I started and which direction I went.

I stopped so I wouldn't get more lost than I already was. I sat on an old tree stump and rested my elbows on my knees to run the argument through my mind. I missed the warmth the fire had been giving off as a chill went through my body. I needed to get back to the campsite. I heard a piece of wood snap. I froze and my back stiffened. Who or what could have made the noise? Could I have imagined it? Maybe the noise was just an animal moving around.

"Well a little girl alone in the woods. Girly, hasn't anyone ever told you not to go off by yourself at night in the middle of the woods?" a strong voice weaved through the trees.

I jumped up to only to have come face to face to a guy's chest. I looked into his face and his eyes seemed familiar. I turned to run only to notice there was another guy with him who was just as large. Both were more built then I was.

"Hey, is it just me or does this girl look familiar?" a raspy voice questioned.

Even through the darkness, I could see the other man's grin as his friend grabbed my arms and held me prisoner against him, so my back was against his chest.

"It's the girl without any manners. Remember? Her Prince Charming tried to hurt us. Well I guess you're lucky, girly. We actually came back to see you like we said we would."

"Go to hell!" I spat then literally spat in the other's face.

He slapped me hard against the cheek. My head whipped to the side.

"Now you really need to learn some etiquette, young lady. And I think my friend and I just might know how to teach you," the stronger voice spoke. He took a pause before continuing. "My friend, do you still have that rope that we used for our last shelter?"

My insides started to become aware of what the two men were hinting at. I tried even harder to get out of the guys arms. His grip tightened to the point where it hurt too much to fight him. I screamed, hoping I hadn't wandered too far from camp for anyone to hear me. Instead of a rescue party coming to get me or even just Aaron, I got a harder slap across the face. My teeth scratched my inner cheek. The guy who had a hold of me threw me onto the ground. I hit my head against a tree as I fell. I felt the bark scraped across my skin.

My vision blurred as I sensed my arms being tied around the tree. A thick wad of cloth was stuffed into my mouth. One of the men brushed against my cheek with a long falsely tender movement that was horribly sinister.

"What a pretty girl. Now you'll learn what happens when you don't use your manners with a real man."

10
Aaron

I woke up to a hazy sort of day. I looked at the bodies lying near me. There were only five. I sat up and scanned the area. Lauren still wasn't with us. It seemed like she hadn't come back at all during the night. She could have gotten lost out there. She could have been waiting for daylight to find her way back. I had to give her some credit that she could have left marks for to find her way back to us. So, I decided to wait a little longer for her before I went into the woods to hunt for her.

By noon, everyone was up and was functioning to the best of their abilities. We all ate a little of what we could find, but still no Lauren. The others were beginning to worry to make comments about Lauren not being there, so I went into the forest to go find her. I put Jill in charge since I never trusted or liked Cole. He seemed barely able to take care of himself let alone two six-year-olds, who had no problem testing their boundaries.

After what seemed like hours, I still couldn't find her. I was just about to turn around when something caught my eye. Lying there limply was a bloody and dirty figure, bent almost in half. I walked closer and realized it was Lauren. I bolted toward her, leaping over whatever was in my way. My heart pounded, each bound echoing in my ears. Lauren didn't seem to be conscious. Her eyes were closed, and her chest barely moved. She was gagged, and her hands were tied together behind the trunk of the tree.

Working quickly, I untied her arms and took the rag out of her mouth. I was afraid to touch her. I looked closer at her wrists that were tied. They were raw with specks of blood dusted across her pale skin. Her long pants were now ripped all the way down to her knees. Her shirt was torn in half in the front.

She was bruised and dried blood dyed her skin. Anger built up in me as I tried to figure out who the hell would do this to anyone. I lifted her head a little, soothingly to get a better glimpse at her face.

"Lauren. Lauren? Please wake up," I whispered to her as I stroked her cheek.

I heard her moan in pain. Hope shot through me as I heard signs of life within her. Slowly, the wounded eyes opened as though her own eye lids had become too heavy for her to move. Her body stirred, bit by bit.

"Aaron?" Her voice was hoarse.

"Yeah, it's me. You're safe now," I answered, caressing her face and brushing stray hair out of her face, I refrained myself from kissing her forehead.

Lauren loosely wrapped her arms around my neck as she shook. I could feel her tears on my shoulders. She moved her head, so my shoulder and neck cradled her face. Slowly and tenderly I put my arms around Lauren, and she whimpered. My heart felt like it was coming apart at the seams.

"What happened?" I asked quietly, nuzzling the top of her head so she wouldn't see the fury building within me.

"Those men… those men… that you saved us from… they… they… raped…"

"Shh… You're safe now." I spoke into her

hair. I put one hand on her back and the other was behind her head. "I'm not going to let anything else bad happen to you. I promise. I'm so sorry..."

Slowly I shifted her so I could pick her up. I carried her to the small creak I heard in the distance. Most of the water was still frozen, but there were parts that had started to thaw.

"This might be cold, Lauren, but we need to wash the blood off you," I whispered as I tried to put her down, but she held on.

"Please, don't leave me." Her voice was small and weak as she spoke against my skin.

Lauren kept her face buried in my neck as she held on. Her grip was weak. She had to be in a lot of pain. She began to shiver. I realized I didn't pick up her sweatshirt that was thrown carelessly on the ground. I made a mental note to grab that on the way back. Slowly, I sat us down by the water and helped her out of what was left of her clothes. I knew we had to fix her clothes because it was too cold to wear the summer clothes that we kept in the backpack just yet.

Soon, I finished cleaning her up, which I knew she would have normally argued against me seeing or touching her nearly naked body if she felt better. Before I put her shirt back on, I grabbed a stick and poked two tiny holes at the bottom and top of her shirt. I then ripped the cloth the men gagged her with and slipped it through the two holes.

I helped her to slip her arms through the arm slots so what used to be the back of the shirt was now the front, then tied the cloths together. I looked at her jeans and knew there wasn't anything I could do to fix those. They were done with and she was going to have to finish winter in her shorts. Slowly I picked her up again and headed back, but I made sure I picked up the sweatshirt before we went back to the group. I sat down on the ground with her to put her sweatshirt on her. She needed to wear it to cover up what seemed like hundreds of scratches and bruises on her arms, back, chest, and most of her body. Her eyes were drifting closed as she kept her head resting on my shoulder.

Being as careful as I could, I walked back to camp with her sleeping in my arms. It took me a little bit, but I finally located the camp as the day seemed to be slipping away again. When I entered the camp, everyone was there so I didn't have to worry about going on another search party. What I didn't think about happening happened. Everyone was gapping at the limp form in my arms and I hadn't thought of story to make up for the horrible truth. As lightly as I could, I laid her down where we had slept the night before, where she should have been if we hadn't argued

"What happened to her?" asked Jill in a panicky whisper.

"I found her in a ditch. She must have fallen in it when she took a walk last night," I spoke, my tone was monotone.

I kept gazing down at Lauren as I brushed a stray hair away from one of her black eyes. I didn't glance up to see if the rest believed my lie or not, but there wasn't a chance I was going to tell them the truth, that she had been beaten and raped. Slowly I laid behind her and placed an arm around her to keep her close without hurting her.

The next morning, I knew we had to leave the area for our own safety. Lauren was still tender, so I carried her in the bridal style again after she had changed into her shorts. I wasn't expecting for us to travel so far with her in my arms. So that meant Sean and Paige's main holders were out of service. Everyone was still silent. No one knew what to say or if they should say anything at all about Lauren's condition. The only noises were coming from Sean and Paige, who didn't seem to know how to be quiet. They were whispering to each other, but I couldn't hear what they were saying as Paige giggled.

There was a rustle in the trees as the wind danced through the woods. The trees waved above us making the shadows shift. That's when I heard a faint crack of a stick. Lauren jolted, then held me tighter around my neck. My heart raced, and I hoped the men weren't following us. I hadn't even thought of that when I rescued her the previous day. We all stopped dead in our tracks. We didn't dare take another step forward.

"You are entering the Lost Boys' land! Go away. You're not wanted!"

I heard a little kid's voice and relaxed. Then I saw the body the voice had come from. There was a little boy around the same age and stature as Sean standing on a rock. He was in jean overalls with a blue shirt. He had a matching blue hat with blond hair underneath that came out under the brim, giving him a scarecrow appearance. A boy identical to that one came over wearing the same jean overalls, but with green shirt and hat instead.

"You two aren't even four feet tall!" Cole barked.

"Watch it, Cole. We don't know if there are adults around," Jill spoke up.

"They said Lost Boys, which is from *Peter Pan*. The Lost Boy's didn't have parents," Mandy said softly.

How did two little boys last this long without parents? We were having enough trouble and there were seven of us working together.

"What did I tell you two?" a voice was heard in the distance a little deeper than the twins.

"Shush, servant, and bow down before us!" yelled one of the twins, he had a tall stick that he banged on the ground he stood on.

That was when another boy came into sight. He was around a foot taller than the two boys and was wearing glasses. His blond hair was darker than the twins and was in complete chaos. He looked between Mandy's and Jill's age.

"Who are you guys?" asked the other

boy, his tone more frustrated with the twins than anything else.

"We're a group passing through. Are there adults with you guys?" I asked.

"No adults. It's just us three. And there isn't anyone near here for miles. Just tons of rocks," the older kid responded. He attempted to get the stick out of the young boy's hand, which only failed and won a tongue stuck out at him.

Great, there wasn't any shelter near here. I shifted Lauren in my arms a little and she winced. The three boys made their way down from the ledge to meet us, so I sat down with Lauren in my lap. When I looked up, the new ones were standing among us.

"So, who are you guys, really?" I asked.

"I'm RJ and these are my little brothers Kyle, blue, and Tony, green. I'd watch out for them if I were you," the older out of the three answered with narrowed eyes on the younger two.

"How old are you guys?" asked a hoarse Lauren.

"I'm eleven, and they're six," RJ answered.

"I'm Lauren, this is Aaron, Mandy, Jill,

Cole, Paige, and Sean," she said, pointing to each person, still sounding tired and hurt. Her hand fell into her lap and I interlaced her fingers in mine.

"Can we join you? I don't think an eleven-year-old should be taking care of his brothers."

My eyes widened at his boldness. I mean, no eleven-year-old should ever have to take care of his little brothers, but he just met us not even five minutes ago. We didn't need more people to look after. Damn it! That was what Lauren was telling me. I looked down at her now as her eyes were open, staring at the three. If we hadn't argued, this wouldn't have happened to her.

That was first time that realization settled in on me. Lauren hadn't said anything yet to blame me for what happened to her. But I knew if we hadn't argued, she wouldn't have gone in the woods by herself. I hated myself when I realized when I said I didn't care what happened to her. My heart sunk down to bottom of my stomach as these rushed. I rubbed her thumb with mine. Lauren had been attacked because of me.

"Aaron. Aaron… Earth to Aaron." I heard a light laugh that snapped me out of my guilt trip.

"Yeah?"

"It's not a big deal if they join us, right?" Lauren asked, looking up into my eyes.

"Um, yeah sure they can."

I couldn't say no in front of the kids; they'd be left alone and would have to defend for themselves. That was just plain evil, heartless, and I especially can't do that in front of a Lauren. I didn't know how they had lasted this long, since we were having so much trouble.

RJ fell over at our feet. "Thank you so much!" he praised, practically bowing before us.

"Is there something you're not telling us?" I asked, a little afraid to know the answer with a raised brow.

"Um… my brothers are a bit on the… I think the right word is difficult side."

"How hard can they be?" Cole asked the same question that was on my mind.

"Just wait and see, if you don't believe me," was all RJ said.

I heard small snickers and turned to look at the twins, who had smirks on their faces. This might have been a bad idea.

"Are you sure this is the right way?" I

asked RJ.

I couldn't believe we were taking directions from these little kids. We were weaving between trees and asteroids as we tried to get out of the woods. Lauren had decided to make an attempt to walk today but was still in pain. I could tell from her facial expressions. Yet she stayed silent through her suffering. I stayed close to her in case she needed support. We hadn't walked far, however, before I picked her up and held her close to me.

"I was fine with walking on my own, thank you very much," Lauren responded, with the last four words stringing together.

"Just humor me, Lauren."

She was calm as we continued our way; it would be a little longer before we stopped again.

We sat around in a close huddle as the twins began staring at Lauren.

"What happen to her?" one of the twins finally asked.

"She fell down," I answered quickly.

"Where did she fall?"

"Into a ditch," I answered, the words shooting out automatically.

Lauren turned to glance at me and raised an eyebrow.

"You realize she is here right?"

Silence hung in the air.

"So, do you two have a plan on where we're going?" asked RJ.

"Well, we were thinking of going west."

"Ha, that is a big mistake there, big guy." A sad smile was on RJ's lips as he shook his head slowly.

"Why?" I asked, afraid to hear what he had to say.

"There isn't anything left west of here. We traveled that way for over a month and found nothing but one big graveyard and rocks with steam coming out of them."

"Yeah, it was cool!" one of the twins yelled, high fiving the other.

"But that jerk wouldn't let us climb on the rocks." the other finished as he turned to glare at his older brother.

The twins then stuck their tongues out at their brother.

"You two aren't very nice," commented Paige while frowning at the twins and holding the stuffed animal close to her chest.

"Being nice isn't fun." spat one of the twins toward Paige.

"You're messed up," Paige answered

with a disgusted face, leaning against me.

Lauren picked Paige up and held the little girl in her lap. Paige wrapped her arms around Lauren, resting her head against Lauren's chest.

The twins laughed.

"How about we stay here tonight to sketch out a new plan? So, are you serious that there's nothing out there?" I asked, watching Lauren next to me with Paige and Sean in her arms.

I hoped that they weren't hurting her by climbing on her.

"It looks like another planet out there. There wasn't anything living or growing over there. There were pieces of rocks, rubble, and people all over the place."

"Should we go back to the house in Pennsylvania?" Lauren was oblivious of the fight between the little ones as she absentmindedly played with Paige's hair.

"You think that it's wise since we were found there once before? Could we even find our way back there?" I asked with a raised brow.

"Wait a minute. You were in a house and you left?" asked RJ, widening his brown eyes.

"We're kind of on the run from someone," I muttered guiltily.

"Great, I've made an alliance with criminals." RJ yelped as he threw his arms up into the air.

"I would answer your question, but he still won't tell me anything about it," answered Lauren.

There wasn't much to tell. "Don't worry it's not as bad as you're probably thinking," I responded with a feeble smirk.

"And when will you be sharing that information?" asked Cole sourly.

"That's what I was thinking," Lauren muttered.

I knew I had to tell Lauren, but I didn't want to just then. I didn't want to watch her face turn from shocked to dismay at me and ultimately to plain disgust. I knew I had to tell her, but I wanted to keep her as a friend longer before she wanted to run and hide from me. Was that so wrong?

"I don't think we went this way," complained Jill sounding annoyed.

"Of course, we did, doesn't that tree look familiar?" I answered, pointing to a tree as Sean mimicked my footsteps.

"You're recognizing trees! We're in the freaking woods and you're basing where we are going on *trees*?" yelled Jill, really ticked off now, her hands held in front of her clenched and shaking.

"Fine, we'll stop here if you're that insecure about where we're going." I almost snapped after a day of walking. We all needed a good night's sleep.

We all sat down on the ground.

"What are the odds of us even finding that house again? I mean, we haven't been to it in months. Something could have happened to the house too."

I stared at Lauren who sat next to me. Her black eye wasn't as deep and dark in color as it had been a few days ago. The healing had left her eye looking closer to normal. Her lips were still swollen and there was still a cut by them. She curled her legs under her to sit on, but she was now in a pair of Jill's capris.

"I think if we got ourselves this far, we should be able to figure out where we came from, right?" I shrugged.

"But we didn't mark anything when we were walking, and I don't think we had a particular path," Lauren answered like the hope had been sucked out of her.

"We didn't, but that doesn't mean we can't figure it out," I responded as I took one of her hands in mine, our fingers interlaced once more. "So, we'll rest up tonight. Do you think you'll be well enough tomorrow to walk?" I asked, looking into her eyes.

"I've been saying that I could walk on my own for days, but you wouldn't listen." Lauren sighed before she narrowed her eyes.

I formed a small grin as I gave her hand a light squeeze.

"Only because I knew you were lying," I replied, leaning my forehead against hers, an unwanted smile formed on her lips, but true none the less.

"Are you two some married couple, boyfriend girlfriend thing or something?" asked the very daring eleven-year-old.

"No!" yelled Lauren and I in unison, jumping away from each other a little before we turned to glance at each other then back at RJ.

"Sure." He rolled his eyes.

"We're seventeen years old." Lauren spoke up as if that should be the obvious answer.

"So, in this world you don't think that

anyone at any age could just claim to be married to someone?" RJ quizzed with a raise brow.

Lauren and I stared at each other, then shook our heads. Yeah, marriage wasn't what we were expecting from each other, well at least not then. Our arguing that night had been a fine example of that. I guess that was another reason she didn't want to have kids with me. I was really beginning to hate her arguments.

"I still can't picture being married at this age," Lauren said.

"Why? People used to get married at one point when the girl was thirteen. They did that because people died younger. Well I don't think people will be living too long nowadays," RJ said.

"Are you trying to make us a married couple?" I finally asked.

"No, it's just how you two treat each other and why else would you guys stay with each other like you guys do if you two weren't together?" RJ continued nonchalantly.

RJ had a good question, and I was a bit taken aback by it.

"To survive, you last longer when you are with a group," I finally answered.

"Like a family?" RJ asked.

"Okay, only a very dysfunctional family." Lauren laughed a little now, her gaze on me.

"There's a scary man," Paige mumbled sitting up.

Lauren titled her head, "There isn't-"

"No, he's over there," Paige voice cried out as she pointed out in the dark.

"Paige, if there was anyone in the woods, I would have heard it. Just go back to sleep. You just had a nightmare," Cole yawned before turning to his other side.

Paige glanced back over to a section of the woods. My own eyes scanned to see what she could be seeing.

"Paige, go back to sleep. We'll keep an eye out," Lauren soothed Paige, stroking her back until she fell asleep.

"How are you feeling?" I whispered to the girl next to me.

Since the attack, Lauren had been sticking closer to me while being a little on edge to the touch. She rested her arms on a fallen log for her head to relax on as she lay on her side so she could face me. Lauren's eyes weren't fully open as she looked up at me.

"Yeah, I'm fine. Why are you asking again?"

"Are you mostly healed now?" I answered with a question.

"Eh for the most part. It's been a bit since that the attack."

It had been a couple weeks later, and we were outside of the town once more, but Lauren had put her foot down about actually going back into the town.

I was just impressed we had gotten so far without a marked trail. Because I felt bad for her, I decided it was best that we stayed out of the wild town.

"What's with the weird questions?" Lauren inquired.

"Asking how you are is a weird question?"

"Only when you ask how much I'm healed, yes then it is weird."

"I guess that is kind of personal question." My voice softened even more.

"Just a bit." She used a weird voice.

I scooted lower so I could be more on her eye level. Her once purely blue, innocent eyes were dimmer as more reality was thrown at her in the past months. She gave me a weak smile, which I returned as I took her hand in mine. Her wrist was still slightly red, so I used gentle touches. I looked up at her again to find that she was closer to me with her eye lids slightly lower.

"It seems when something goes wrong, it only happens to me," she whispered sleepily.

"A good portion of the stuff that does happen, happens to you. Remember I was shot in the arm?" I questioned her; my thumb rubbed hers.

"The bullet just grazed your arm, it wasn't much."

I raised an eyebrow and looked at her straight in the eyes.

"You only say that because it wasn't your arm."

Lauren smiled a little more as her eyes grew heavier. I curled up next to her as she lifted her head. She shifted her head so that she could rest it on my shoulder. I wrapped an arm around her as I leaned my head against the top of her head. I started to close my eyes and listened to her breathing as the two of us fell asleep.

11

Lauren

I shifted a little as I tried to go back to sleep and curled closer toward the warmth that was against me. When I realized there wasn't any way I was going to fall back to sleep, I kept my eyes closed and stretched to take the time to at least unwind. I extended my arms and legs as I yawned, but then changed my mind and went back to sleep anyway... or tried.

"Awake?"

I opened my eyes slowly to adjust to the light around us, but it wasn't as sunny today as I peeked over to see Aaron. He was partially awake as well and peering down at me. Okay we were a little too close for comfort and shouldn't be acting like this with this the little kids around. I know we were just lying next to each other, but our gestures seemed so natural together.

"We should probably get a move on," I said in order to get us up so we could put some space between us.

I started to wake everyone up, and then we were on our way. Sean was on my back. He leaned his head into the back of my neck while Paige did the same to Aaron to get some extra sleep. They needed sleep more than we did. While Tony and Kyle were running in every direction, their brother RJ just watched them while sticking with Cole, who didn't look pleased to have a follower.

"So, this place we're going to is an actual house?" asked RJ.

"Yes, it is."

"If you guys were in an actual house, why did you leave?"

"Safety reasons mostly," Aaron answered. "Didn't we already go through this?"

"Is it just me or has it gotten a hell of a lot darker out here all of the sudden?" asked Cole.

I stopped and stared up, noticing the change of weather too. The haze that was about when we woke up had disappeared to be taken over by very dark sky. Hues of green and red stretched as far as the eye could see.

"Maybe it is going to rain?" suggested Mandy nervously, her voice shaking.

Sudden, intense heat swarmed around us as the earth began to shake slowly at first but started to increase. My body started to tremble as déjà vu hit. Aaron and I turned our heads, so our eyes locked as realization and panic kicked in.

"Run!" We both yelled after we found our voices. Then we took off.

We all started to run as rocks the size of cars, were hurled from the sky toward us. We tried to stick together, while running as a cluster. This way no one would get left behind as it seemed the rocks were following us with each step we took. Rocks landed to our right and in front of us as we scrambled and screamed. We hoped we would live through this. The earth below my feet gave way with to the violent pulse of the ground and asteroids.

A screech escaped my lips as I fell, and Sean rolled forward with the others. A huge hole formed in the ground, tearing the world in two, as I struggled to find something to grab on to. I spotted some pathetic roots and grabbed on. I knew the plant would not hold, but I needed to try to get back up and out of the hole. I heard more shrieks and I glanced down to see who had caused the noise, to see who else had fallen. Glimpsing down I could see little Mandy who was slipping farther down. Her big brown eyes were filled with utter alarm as her little hands tried to grab onto something, but there wasn't anything.

"Mandy!"

There wasn't anything she could grasp onto as she continued to fall down into the darkness. Her cries became faint through the sounds of the world that tried to finish us off. Tears streamed down my face as I wondered when I would join her. I could feel the roots that I had a grasp on unthreading from the earth because of my weight. I didn't think I could handle watching the world above me disappear.

The second the roots were about to let go; something took hold of my wrist. I looked up to see Aaron hanging over the edge, trying to pull me up. Just like when Aaron had done when he helped us out of my basement all those months ago.

"Lauren, give me both of your hands!" Aaron shouted with something in his eyes. Terror?

I stared into a blood-red sky that was speckled with black asteroids. I grabbed both of his hands and hoped to get out of this mess soon. Aaron started to strain as he tried to pull me up, but he lacked good enough support to bring both of us back up.

"Please, Aaron!"

I knew I couldn't hold the tears back. I knew if I died Sean would be alone. I couldn't leave them. Yet I watched Aaron try to get back up and I knew there was little hope for him to be able to save both of us and I tried to speak, but nothing came out. I tried again in an attempt to sound tough.

"Let go!" I yelled so that Aaron could hear me over the chaos around us.

Aaron's blue eyes widened in pure shock as his irises locked onto mine.

"Are you nuts? I'm not going to let go of you! I can get us back up!" he shouted over the commotion; he was stubborn.

I watched Aaron struggle as he tried even harder to pull us up. His body tightened with all his strength as the terrain below him began to shudder. Tears gushed down my face. I stared into Aaron's eyes as they showed determination at getting both of us out. I remembered a time those very same eyes never even glanced my way and now all they seemed to do was watch me. I seemed to be all his eyes could hold onto, which made my heart skip a beat.

"This has to be done…"

I began to loosen my grip on his hands as I tried to seize back the swelling in my throat to show that I knew what I was doing.

"Lauren, no!" Aaron begged.

My skin began to slip out of his hands and just when I thought I'd be falling to my death Aaron grabbed onto my wrists so tight that it was excruciating. Gradually, Aaron pulled me up until we were both standing on the unstable ground. I nearly fell into his arms as an asteroid landed besides us. Aaron and I grabbed Sean and Paige before we made our way toward the others. The ground kept rumbling as I scrutinized my footing and took off.

The trees around us fell as a bolt of lightning struck them and limbs burst into flames. Jill and Cole were holding onto Tony and Kyle as we tried to run in another direction. RJ stumbled and, as I turned around to help him, a tree fell onto his back. I was frozen just like poor little RJ. His body was bent badly under the log.

Cole grabbed me by my arm and pulled

me in the direction of the others. We kept running, hoping that we would find some relief, but things kept getting worse with the weather. The sky was dark crimson; veins of light reflected off the asteroids raining down.

We finally came upon an old house that was disheveled with a storm cellar on the side. I could see Aaron a little ahead of us, trying to open the thing. Finally, he grabbed a rock and smashed the lock open.

I grabbed Paige and Sean as I rushed down the cellar with the others, my heart racing. I heard the metal doors being slammed shut as Aaron raced down with us. Together, we curled up in a corner to wait for all of this to end. The four little ones curled up close to me as I hid my face on the top of one of their heads, wishing it could all end. Tears kept pouring down my face not knowing whether I should even be happy to be alive during all of this or should be wishing I were dead.

"How are we going to live through this?" I whispered in Aaron's ear.

"We're going to live through this the same way we've made it this long."

"Dumb luck?" I asked, my voice shaking.

He gave a light laugh in my ear.

"No, it's because we stick together even if there's an argument."

The house above us trembled like my heart. I couldn't help but think of the two missing faces we would never see again. I wondered, if we lived through this, how we would get by. The twins watched their older brother, their only remaining family member, get taken away from them — die in front of them.

Then there was the little, sweet Mandy whose face I could still see falling into the darkness as I hung there in the red light. I remembered babysitting her every first weekend of the month as her parents helped at church. She and I would play board games or dress up as she did my hair. She was the nice youngster, an only child, and wanted to play with all the neighborhood children because she was nice to everyone. Now she was dead, and I was alive, and I wished it were the other way around.

More tears ran down my face as the earth shook less and the loud crashes decreased. The house was still shaking as the storm calmed down and I hoped the place wouldn't come crashing in on us. I held the younger ones tighter as we were enveloped in an eerie silence.

Aaron slowly stood up as the rest of us

shuddered in the corner. I really wished I could just seize his hand to stop him from walking away from us. Instead, I sat there watching his broad shoulders and lean muscular back as he headed toward the cellar's doors just to open them a crack. He closed the heavy doors once more as he tried to make sure the metal wouldn't slam down hard.

"We'll stay here for a bit," he said, his usually strong, deep voice wavering.

Aaron curled up with us as we tried to calm down and forget all that had happened. My nerves got the best of me as I fell asleep, the entire night nightmares caused me to be restless.

Sleeping sitting up was not a good idea. I tried to move without waking the others up, but I couldn't do so comfortably. Shifting was going to be troublesome. I sat with four little ones, who used me as a pillow. I tried to move my limbs a little to get comfortable, but I couldn't. I really needed to get up myself, I was stiff as muscles begged to be in motion. Slowly, I moved the younger ones a little so I could stand up. I started to stretch my muscles and crack my back when I noticed Aaron standing quietly by the door. There was a sliver of light coming in through the cracks in the door, giving me just enough light to see him.

I took careful steps over to him. I stopped when I was behind him and hesitantly put a hand on his shoulder. He just as tentatively wrapped his arm around me, so his hand rested on my hip, without having to turn to see that it was me who touched him. The images of Mandy and RJ started to roll in front of my eyes like a movie, and I tried to block them out. I closed my eyes and turned my face into his shoulder.

"Why is this happening? She was so young!" I muttered as I tried to not wake the others.

I could feel a tear or two escape my eyes and slip down onto Aaron's shoulder. With a tender touch, he pulled up my chin slightly so that I could gaze into his eyes. I could see that Aaron was in just as much pain as I was. He leaned his forehead against mine soothingly and I stared into his deep blue eyes. Unsure as to why I was doing so I titled my head up so that my lips could briefly touch his.

I didn't bother really to pull away as I felt Aaron stay as well. Gradually, Aaron pressed his lips little by little onto mine. I closed my eyes as

I gave into the kiss. The kiss was a way to escape and bring some peace to me even if the calmness was just for a moment. My lips began to be in motion with his in their slow teasing, yet loving gesture. After everything we had been through, we just needed to know that the other was still there, alive. Carefully I wrapped my arms around his neck to hold Aaron close to my body as his long, blond hair brushed against the skin on my face.

Without being rough, Aaron's tongue glided over my lips as they asked for entrance, which I allowed without a second thought. My hand slid up his neck unhurriedly to his hair just to skim the edge of his earring before tangling in his hair. Aaron's once thin, silky, light blond hair now was dirty and matted as I felt the strands interweave in my fingers. However, the texture didn't bother me. Aaron's hot tongue intertwined with mine as my blood seemed to have turned on fire. I stood on my toes ever so slightly to bring Aaron even closer to me.

A gun shot loudly, whistling out into the air to rip us apart. We both stared, wide eyed, searching for the source. A few loud voices were coming closer to the storm cellar's doors as Aaron and I raced to the others in order to hide.

Everyone was awake now in the huddle.

"Is Mr. Manson still looking for the boy?" a voice on the other side asked.

"He's convinced he's still alive," another male voice responded next to the other.

"How can the kid still be alive? Barely anyone lived through the second storm!"

"He's really out for the boy."

"The world is still too big to look for just one person, and now without any of the technology that was working before the second storm there's no chance we'll even find the boy."

"Dean Manson has had men on this boy's trail and knows the area he is in."

"That is why we're here?"

"You finally caught on!"

I held Sean and Paige tighter to me as the people started to bang on the doors. I hadn't realized Aaron had put a bar through the handles. I couldn't believe I had let my guard down for a brief moment for a stupid kiss. A great but a stupid kiss none the less. Now we were going to get caught because of our foolishness. My heart was racing, and I turned my head to look over my shoulder to peek over at Aaron to see him grab something and then creep over to the doors. Before I could do anything to stop him, Aaron ran out and shut the doors behind him.

12
Aaron

Standing tall and ready, I swung the bat at one of the men. The other jumped after hearing the metal bat collide with his companion. I stood there, ready to hit again as the other was reaching for something. That was when I remembered they had a gun. Their gun fire was what had separated Lauren and me in the first place. I acted quickly as I swung the bat into the guy's shoulder. While the two were on the ground, I planned to go back down into the cellar to be with the others, but I wasn't quick enough.

Hands were tightly wrapped around my shoulders to pull me backward as I struggled to get free, twisting every which way so that I could fight the offender away. I couldn't get caught; there was too much depending on me right now. It wasn't just my life anymore. There were also the lives of the children in the cellar, who had more than just grown on me. Then there was Lauren.

I thrashed around as I strived to get away from my capturer.

"Stop it, you piece of crap!" a voice growled.

I was pushed onto the ground roughly as I rolled over onto my back with hopes of getting off the ground before the men came at me again. Unfortunately, one of their boots had other plans as its owner kicked me in the side. I groaned as I tensed, looking up just to see third party hover over me. There, standing tall and proud with a smirk on his face, was Mr. Dean Manson himself.

I moaned as I came into consciousness, my mind still swirling around. I tried to put the pieces together as many scenes spun around in circles within my mind. I tried to figure out what was going on. My hand went to my throbbing head which felt like it was being torn in two.

"I told them it wasn't necessary to hit

you, but you know, they just couldn't help themselves," a strong voice said matter-of-factly.

"Yeah, I'm sure you really cared about me getting smacked in the head," I muttered, trying to comprehend what his followers had hit me with, something heavy and solid.

The bat I had? It sounded reasonable. Maybe I got another kick to the head? I blinked a few times to get my vision straight.

"You look a lot different from when you got me arrested," Manson spoke nonchalantly.

I stared up at him; I couldn't figure out if I should be afraid or furious. What kind of comment was that anyway? Was that supposed to be an insult? Or was he just stating a fact from everything that everyone had been through.

"I didn't get you arrested. You got yourself arrested," I snapped.

He smirked, but without the same gleam in his eyes he possessed only a moment a before.

"You had some help with that, but you're not as much of a hero people make you out to be," Manson continued carelessly.

The embarrassment of the event started to resurface. If I didn't need to keep my guard up, I would have glanced away in guilt.

"So, how many of you are there?"

I raised an eyebrow at him because I did not understand what he could possibly mean.

"What are you talking about?"

His happiness returned as he sneered down at me.

"The girl from the cabin is with you. I know that much. And there are some others, I don't know though is exactly how many there are with you. The numbers seemed to keep changing. Poor pathetic souls just don't know what they got themselves into."

My muscles tightened as he mentioned the others.

"I have no idea what you are talking about," I responded, refraining from speaking through gritted teeth.

His gray eyes darkened like a horrible tornado was approaching.

"She's such a lovely girl. It's a shame to put her to waste like that. To have her wander the woods to get dirty and starve to near death." His voice was even, but I could not take the bait.

"I don't know who you're talking about. I travel alone."

"There were a few other little children, one that the girl seemed especially fond of, a brother possibly?" Manson's voice rose at the end to fulfill the question.

I aimed to keep the poker face as my insides were on fire with rage. Dean Manson had better not touch them or he was a dead man!

"I can tell by your body language you are very fond of the girl." His words were smooth as he talked and stood up to walk closer to me. "I'll make you a deal, Aaron. You give your life to me, and I'll make sure the girl has a roof over her head for the rest of her life."

I glared up into his stormy eyes as his dark brown beard formed around his evil grin. I couldn't have hated anyone more then I hated this so-called man in front of me. I had to escape from him and to get back to them if I wasn't already too late.

"Oh, don't worry your tiny mind. We haven't touched your little friends." Manson spoke as if he could read my mind. "We just have them surrounded by men with guns. We're actually not far from the abandoned house, if it helps settle your nerves in the slightest bit. It pays to be powerful and have people fear you."

Glaring daggers at him, I stared at the man who circled me while I sat on a cheap card table chair. I tried to formulate a getaway plan as I sat there and waited for him to attack.

"I know I've said before I wanted to get you, that I couldn't wait to get back at you, but I think I have a better plan. The old, 'use the ones they love,' card. Now, before this whole mess, I would have used your parents, well your foster parents. That isn't an option now since they're both dead, yet I can see by just observing you that there are other ones you care for. Oh, yes, I can see your eyes betraying you as I speak. Specks of fear are shining through," Manson taunted.

I began to panic, not realizing how much this guy could read people. I'd noticed his power over people, especially when I had to go to court to be a witness. I'm usually strong willed, but now it wasn't just me and he knew it.

"I'll keep you here to rot forever as I take the girl to be mine, to be a follower of mine, or even as my wife perhaps?"

I couldn't take it anymore. Not only did he have few inches on me, but he was also solid. He pushed me against a wall and knocked the wind out of me. Recovering fast, I nailed him in the face. I grabbed Manson's shoulders to ram my knee into his lower stomach and then ran for the door as he fell over.

Dean Manson let out a frustrated roar as

he attempted to get up. I pushed through the door as the few men in the hall jumped out in order to stop me. My heart raced as I shoved through the men while they stuck their arms out to get a hold of me. Barely escaping, I ran down the stairs from the second floor to the first. A gun shot blared as a bullet skidded into the wall next to me. Nearly falling down the stairs as I sprinted, the front door came into view as stomps and shouts sounded right behind me. They were hot on my trail.

More voices echoed from another part of the building. I flew out the door, darting down the steps and skipping half of the stairs, practically leaping. There was nothing but flat farming land around here. So, if we were to escape, we wouldn't have anywhere close to hide. I rushed around to the back of the house to see a crowd of angry men with guns, and I knew there wasn't much hope in me taking care of them at that moment. The odds were truly against me on that.

With a curse under my breath, I jogged down the field to wait until they left so that I could save the others. I saw the barn was not too much farther, and I picked up my pace. Out of breath, I clenched the barn doors, and with a great deal of pulling, I finally got the door open enough so that I could slip in. Though the hiding spot was obvious and may not have been very safe, I was able to keep an eye on them until I was ready to go release the others.

The men wandered through the fields, waiting for me to come out. My heart thumped against my ribs and began to beat faster to a new rhythm as I tried to figure out a plan to get out of here without being stupid. I couldn't fail, I thought as an adrenaline rush kicked in and I slid toward the ground. Crouching through the overgrown plants, I made my way out of the barn. The tall wild plants kept me hidden as I proceeded back near the house.

I knew this wasn't the smartest thing to do, but it had to be done right away. When I got close to the house, I stopped. I observed as the men paced around with their hands on their guns, ready to shoot me without a second thought. I stared at the broken porch thinking if I could just get to the hole without getting myself killed, I would be one step closer to the others.

If I could get to the porch, maybe I would be able to dig under the porch to get to the cellar. Could it possibly be that easy to just tunnel through that to get to the group? I mean wouldn't there be cement and stuff? At this moment that was the only option I had, and I was going to take it. I just had to wait for the right opportunity to get to the porch. I mean, how long could they possibility stand there waiting for me?

Okay so those men really had no life or no better orders, I thought as the hung moon high in the sky. The specks of stars and a glowing moon were inspecting the scene almost eagerly to see what would happen. The night wasn't what it used to be as I tried to wait for the men to give up and just let me get to the stupid porch so I could save my family! Finally, the men started to go inside so there were fewer men on watch. I hoped I wouldn't have to wait much longer.

Two of the men began to talk to each other and I figured if I didn't break for it then, I might never get the chance. One of the men started to laugh as I bolted quietly to the broken cave of a porch. The area felt cramped beneath the dark porch. I had to swat my hands around the dirt to find something that I might have been able to use as a shovel. I knew this plan was unrealistic, but I had to try.

I groped around on the floor to find something that I could use until I found a piece of wood that might have been a board of the porch at one point and started to hack at the ground without bringing attention to myself with the shelter around me. I could feel the dirt and rocks move bit by bit as I assaulted the ground. I started to broaden the hole. I knew I had to be able to fit people through the gap.

I tried to move faster in my attempt to remove the ground. The faster I moved the more that I knew I looked like a lunatic, but I was determined to get to the others to get away from this place. We needed to flee from the murderous Dean Manson, and we had to do so quickly. The wood dulled as I attempted to shift more dirt and rocks until I hit the wood too hard and the plank shattered.

After cursing under my breath, I crawled into the partial hole to dig with my hands. Clawing at the ground like an animal made my hands hurt as I felt the ground tear at my skin in rebellion. Dirt was getting jabbed under the already jagged stubs of my fingernails. I hoped the cellar was near. It was amazing that no one heard me. Perhaps the followers were waiting

243

for me with a trap in the cellar.

The ground started to thin, and I stopped. I moved a little. I kept my head low so that I wouldn't bump it on the floor of the porch and put my feet at the bottom of the hole. Using as much force as I could, I kicked the bottom of the hole until it gave a little under the soles of my sneakers. One last kick and the bottom of the hole gave way. Working fast, I knew I had to hurry because someone must have heard the dirt below fragmenting as loose cement fell onto the ground.

I swung into the dark quiet cellar. Finally, I spotted the dark shapes in the corner. I made my way over there. I tapped one of them on the shoulder, which make her jump and nearly scream. I pressed my hand against Jill's mouth until realization took over.

"It's just me. Are we all here?" I asked squinting in the dark.

I tried to figure out how many bodies were there, but it seemed like few were missing. I noticed the heights of the lumps in the shadows.

"Mr. Manson… he has Lauren and Sean. Mr. Manson almost got a hold of Paige too, but I was able to get her away and those runts almost got themselves killed!" Jill started out worried and then ended being furious at Tony and Kyle.

I seriously wished I could go back in time and kick myself for allowing them to join us.

"Damn it," I whispered as I stared at the ceiling above me.

I could hear the shuffling of a set of feet in motion above my head. Manson always seemed to be one step ahead of me, no matter what it was. I had to catch up and stop him from doing so. Manson had known I would come down there to get them, not that doing so wasn't an obvious plan, but he also had Lauren and her brother. He didn't seem to be interested in the others and he had found out that those two were the closest to me. Manson even tried to get Paige, who was very attached to me.

"You guys take the little ones out of the hole I came through and I'm going to go try to get the other two from inside. We will meet in the barn out back. I want you to try everything in your power to avoid getting caught."

Jill just nodded as she dragged the others near the opening. As I stood in my spot, I had trouble trying to figure out how to get up inside to save Lauren and Sean. Yet, I knew Manson would be waiting for me, since he seemed to have thought of every situation, I could have used to get in. After cursing to myself again, I crept toward the hole, hoping that the group was long gone. I jumped up and crawled through the outlet to find that I was alone underneath the porch.

Lying on my stomach, I crept toward the edge of the porch using my forearms. As I got to the frame, I saw the barn doors being closed in the distance while the same two men guarding the house. One leaned against the house as they spoke to each other. Working quickly and silently, I made my way to the front door. Using the most obvious way might throw Manson off, but then I saw a semi broken wicker chair just sitting by the edge of porch. I noticed right near the roof there was a window that was open just a crack. I smiled with some hope that I could use this.

Moving fast, I stepped on the creaking chair and jumped up to grab onto the roof before the chair could break. Pretending I was doing the fitness test, I did a pull up to get myself onto the roof so I could swing my legs over and I worked myself over to the window. I wrapped my fingers on the bottom of the sill and tried to lift the glass up. The window seemed stuck as I heaved even harder. The window finally opened. I bent as I swung one leg over and walked into the empty room. I tiptoed toward the door of the dusty, shadowy chamber.

There were a handful of men and a few women grouped together on the couches and chairs in the room next to the one I was in. I could see through the door as it was jarred. I turned my head to glance in the other direction and noticed Lauren sitting on the rim of a bed in another room with Sean in her lap wrapped tightly in her arms. A boom of laughter came from the other room as I rushed toward Lauren before I could get caught.

I moved swiftly as I went through the door to see them sitting there. Lauren's eyes went wide as Sean nearly screamed at the sight of me. Lauren covered Sean's mouth before he could say anything. She followed me out back to the other room before anyone could get to us.

I helped Lauren out of the window as Sean clung onto my back. We got off the roof and sprinted for dear life toward the barn to join the others. I kept thinking that we got escaped way too easy, but I ran harder anyway.

13

Lauren

I stood rocking a bit, clenching Sean close to my chest. My eyes were closed, and I tucked his head under my chin. My body trembled frantically. I didn't know what to do. I felt sick to my stomach like never before.

"Lauren. Lauren, are you okay?" Aaron finally asked, his voice full of concern.

I couldn't even look at him as Dean Manson's words continued to ring through my ears. That was when I felt Aaron's large, calloused hands grab my shoulders, forcing me to stop my swaying and to look at him. I stared into his deep, sapphire eyes, which were wide with fear as they locked onto mine. My stomach felt ten times worse gazing into his expressive eyes.

"Did he hurt you or Sean?" Aaron questioned slowly; his eyes still stayed on mine.

I couldn't speak because I was afraid, I would start crying, so I just shook my head. I knew my voice would betray me.

"Can we please just leave here, now?" I asked feebly.

I felt his arms around my shoulders, holding me securely to him. I closed my eyes and kept them clamped shut, anxious that they would spill their secrets about what had really happened in the house. And what would happen not too far into the future.

"I'm being smooshed!" Sean squeaked as he squirmed. Aaron took Sean from my arms, but I wanted to hold on longer.

The feeling of Sean out of my arms made my hands start to quiver. My hands wouldn't stop trembling as if a black hole had just formed there to take Sean away from me to never be with me again.

"Lauren! What's wrong?" Aaron spoke in a freaked-out tone.

Aaron pulled me to him and stared down at me. I just wanted to be held in his arms and know this was all a nightmare, that our families weren't actually dead and were just waiting at home for us. Yet I knew that his soothing voice would not tell me such a thing. No matter how many nights I wished upon the stars.

After he grabbed a blanket from behind him and wrapped it around me, Aaron lifted me up and sat on the ground with his arms wrapped securely around me. I looped my arms around his shoulders as I edged closer to him. I leaned my face into the base of Aaron's neck. I couldn't bear to lose any more of them—my new family. I couldn't live if I had to watch more of them die.

With a tender touch, Aaron's face rested against the top of my head as he closed his arms tighter around me. He rubbed my back, trying to figure out a way to calm me down. I knew I was scaring Aaron. I was scaring myself as well, but I couldn't help it. I had images of the ones I loved dying before me, I felt helpless. I turned my head slightly to glimpse up at the new one person in my life; Aaron's intense blue eyes explored my own.

Stretching, I placed his lips against mine for a mere touch without any pressure before I went back to my place at the bottom of his neck. I didn't care if the others were watching.

"Can we please go now?" I inquired, my

voice wavering a bit.

Aaron didn't even answer. He simply lifted me and helped me onto my feet. We fled into the night, away from the barn and its home. I held Sean's hand as he held Paige's and Aaron had an arm around my shoulder when our pace slowed. I knew that Aaron was anxious to know if I had lost my mind or something. I soaked up the silence while the thoughts swirled through my mind as I strived to figure out what I was supposed to do.

I mean what Dean Manson had proposed was horrible, and he had been asking for something unreasonable, right? To go with him and he'd forget about Aaron, thus leaving my family with Aaron. Or else, he'd hunt every one of us down to kill us slowly and painfully.

I turned to peek at Aaron under my eyelashes, but his attention was up ahead to get us toward safety, not realizing it wouldn't help at all. I had asked if I could bring the others with me, especially Sean and Paige since they were so young, if I did agree to be with Dean Manson. He of course said no as he claimed they'd be fine with Aaron, at least he wouldn't kill them. My heart ached as I glanced at Sean and Aaron knowing I'd be leaving them. My brother. I was the last real person in our family that would be there for him. I hoped Paige and Aaron would take good care of him when I left.

Aaron was the only guy that I had really cared about. He stayed with all of us even though we weren't his problem. Not only that, but Sean and Paige had bonded with him. Then there were the feelings I had been feeling for him for months now.

I couldn't sit back and watch the whole group die. I paid attention to the direction we headed so I could find my way back to Manson. I knew Aaron was going to be furious with me when he found out. I also knew Aaron would try to think of a way to save us all, but I knew there wasn't any other way.

Finally, we came to a stop in a thick growth of trees. There we all sat in silence, but I knew their eyes were on me, just waiting for me to lose my composure again. I had to wait for them to fall asleep so I could leave. We all sat near one another as I felt everyone's eyes on me, trying to figure out if they were able to talk or not. I had to make things comfortable or they wouldn't go to sleep.

"Is everyone alright?" I asked, scanning around the group.

All of them looked tired and scruffy just being there. The cluster of people before me no longer looked like children. Age and wisdom beyond their years lay in all their haunting eyes. Was I taking the cowardly way out of this life?

"We're all fine, but the question is, are you?" asked Cole.

"I'm fine. I'm sorry, I was just a little spooked." I shrugged.

I glanced at all of them, except for Aaron. I thought he might see right through my act. Out of everyone, Aaron was the one I couldn't fool.

"Are you sure?" Aaron asked.

I turned toward Aaron and nodded my head with my eyes closed. I gave a false smile as real as I could have mustered.

"They didn't hurt me there. Being in there with Manson and his followers just spooked me is all, like I said earlier. Let's just move on and try to make the best of the situation. I mean, we escaped the man who has been after us for months now."

I wanted to have some chance of being happy with everyone before I left them. If I didn't leave that night or early the next morning, Dean Manson would be on the war path for us and there was no chance our little group could win against him.

"I'm just saying we just escaped the man who wants us dead. We should just have a relaxing night for once."

Aaron was now bluntly staring at the dirt we were sitting on and as he played with the overgrown grass between his fingertips that was greening with spring approaching. His legs were crossed, and his once dark blue jeans were torn in places, with dirt embedded into the fabric. The black jacket was zipped up most of the way, hanging a bit on his broad shoulders like on a hanger, but the material seemed to have kept him warm while his shirt underneath was well hidden. I didn't even remember him picking that jacket up.

"Lauren, I'm cold," Paige timidly whispered as she was falling asleep.

"Lauren and I will go get some wood. Jill you're in charge," Aaron responded as he stroked the top of Paige's head.

Aaron stood up and put out a hand to help me up. Aaron pulled lightly to get me off the ground while pulling me closer to him.

"Why is Jill in charge again? I'm older than her!" Cole whined.

I noticed that Aaron's eyes didn't leave

mine as Cole spoke, but they weren't holding any of the loving magic anymore. Aaron's gaze seemed like he was trying to read me instead.

I just started to head in a direction, feeling his hands leave mine. I knew that Aaron was following me as I heard the crunch of the earth below his feet. We stayed by the camp so that we could see everyone, and I picked up pieces of fallen wood. I stood back up, watching Aaron. He appeared beaten, like he had already lost everything. Almost like he knew I was already gone.

"Aaron, what's wrong?" I finally asked, not able to take the silence between the two of us.

I staggered closer to Aaron, hearing the ground cracking beneath my feet.

"I just thought I lost you and Sean to that man," a crushed voice came out.

I gave a half smile as my heart sped up. I pushed some of his hair away from his eyes. I returned my eyes to his, which seemed to never have left my face as much as I had been avoiding his.

"What?" I questioned, smiling.

"When he had me, all he talked about was how he was going to use Sean and you to get to me. That he knew that I—" Aaron paused only for a moment. "He knew that I had feelings for you."

My heart's beating just came to a halt. I felt tears coming to surface with the lump growing in my throat.

"What… What feelings?" I asked, my voice wavering.

Aaron smirked as he leaned his forehead down against mine while his arms wrapped around my waist tenderly.

"Do you really need to ask?"

I didn't know what to say. I had just hoped that I was the only one that cared so this escape could be easier, but I was wrong, so very, *very* wrong. That is why Manson wanted me, Aaron cared for me and my departure would kill Aaron or draw him in.

My eyelids locked to hold back the tears but failed as two escaped. Quickly, I looped my arms around his neck, hoping he hadn't seen them. Yet he must have known he backed up just to glide my face near his. With my face between his hands, he used his thumbs to brush away my slow tears.

"Why are you crying?" Aaron's face was full of concern as his eyes investigated mine. I put on a weak smile.

"Happy tears," I answered.

Half of his mouth turned up in a smile. Aaron pushed back a loose curl behind my ear with a soft whisper of a touch. My heart was screaming out in anguish as my mind was howling that I had to leave him to save his life.

"We probably should get some wood before the others freeze." I wanted to hit myself for saying this, but it was going to be hard enough already.

I wasn't going to make it more difficult by mistreating them right before I left. Why did Aaron have to like me? I never flirted with him or gave him a reason to.

Aaron grinned then locked lips with me, having a hand behind my head with the other on my hip. At first, Aaron kept me close, hungrily pressed against him, but then he pulled away to pick up some wood, leaving me shocked and feeling the need to hit him, yet desiring more.

"We'll talk more when the others are asleep." Aaron's voice sounded like velvet as he sauntered away with the biggest grin on his face.

The little ones were sound asleep along

with Jill. Cole was half asleep since he still didn't trust Aaron to be alone with me by the fire. Since the night I 'fell into a ditch,' it was clear Cole blamed Aaron for what happened to me. My heart was racing as it felt the clock ticking.

My eyes were focused on the dancing flames in front of me. The seasons had been changing around us, but the nights were still cold and made me miss my long pants. This would be my last night spent on the ground and yet I'd rather sleep on the dirt and rocks for the rest of my life than the bed I was promised.

"There's this one song I can remember my foster parents dancing to." Aaron broke the silence after he wrapped an arm around my shoulders.

I peeked at him, attempting to figure out where he was taking the conversation. I hadn't known Aaron was adopted. I had heard of a rumor that had circulated through school about him having foster parents, but I thought it was just high school gossip.

"Every once in a while, they would slow dance to this one song by my mom's garden…" His voice was getting quieter as he spoke.

I leaned back against his chest, finding comfort as he spoke. His head was against mine.

Aaron stood up slowly, pulling me along with him. I realized what he wanted and looped my arms around his neck while his encircled his around my waist. I rested my head against his shoulder. We swayed with his voice reaching my ears made and I smiled as I held back tears.

His deep male voice whispered into my ear like a lullaby as I beamed.

This was one of my favorite songs of all time. It was *Everything I do I do it for you* by Bryan Adams. The lyrics were sappy and yet everything every girl wanted to hear. My school always played it at the school dances and I never had anyone to dance with until now.

Aaron's voice was dying down a bit as I planted my lips on his before he could continue more of the song. Aaron's lips pressed harder, begging for more from me. One of Aaron's hands rested on my lower back pressing me closer to him, to keep me there as my hands drove into his hair. Aaron's tongue met mine only for a moment as I pulled away with grin. I sat on the ground glowing at his shocked face.

"That was for earlier," I sang with a giggle.

Then it was his turn to smile as he started to chuckle. One of Aaron's hands came up and ran through his hair as he laughed. Aaron dropped down to his knees. Aaron got closer to me and tilted my head gently up to capture my smiling lips with his. My mind started to scream at me. This had to end—this was going the opposite direction that I should be allowing it. Things were being taken much too far. I was supposed to be leaving soon not smooching Aaron.

I shoved Aaron back on the ground, and he fell over with ease from surprise. Aaron started to grin seductively at me which made my heart run madly.

"We have to end this before we go too far. There are several little kids here," I ordered, suddenly nervous.

Aaron's eyes were deep and full of lust and never left mine.

"So, you pin me to the ground like this?" He raised an eyebrow. "Someone might think this would be the opposite step. Some might even consider this be taking things farther."

I knew he was right. I was about to get up when he flipped the both of us over, so he was the one on top leaving me pinned to the ground. Again! This is the second time he had me pinned below him.

"And this isn't any different?" I asked. A giggle escaped. I cursed that giggle.

Aaron was smirking down at me then bent down to press his lips to mine. Just to come up so his lips would move against mine as he spoke.

"Only difference being I have no dirty intentions like you."

I rolled my eyes at him as he slid next to me, starting to fall asleep. I crawled into his arms as I closed my eyes, pretending to be asleep as he began to fall into a deep slumber for real. It was a bit until I thought he could possibly be asleep.

"Aaron... Aaron?" I whispered, testing if he was asleep or not.

Aaron didn't even stir, so I tried getting up. Just as I moved, he turned a little in his sleep to where I had been, seeking the warmth that was there a moment ago. My eyes stung. I glanced at little Sean near the twins and Paige. I crept over to Sean and kissed his forehead as I headed off into the night with my arms crossed firmly over my chest, biting down on my lips. I trudged through the night, trying to make as little noise as possible. We hadn't traveled too far from where Dean Manson was located, so I was able to find my way easily. On my march there, I aimed to stay emotionless and not think of the people I had just left behind. I never looked back, but my eyes were moist.

My insides died with each step I took, drawing the house nearer. I wasn't going to let that man see my tears. I needed to be able to keep a little of my pride. I quickened my pace, noticing the sun would rise soon. I was running for dear life to get to that door before the sun did. I was sprinting to my end and I knew it. I banged on the door and pulled my arms more into the sweatshirt to watch the horizon of the sun extending. I became anxious, sensing that I would be caught with the enemy. I whirled back to the door as it swung open to a smirking Dean Manson.

"Ah yes, hello, Lauren. It's nice of you to join us. Now do come in." Manson stepped aside for me to come in.

I turned to look at him. Something hard came crashing to my head as the world around me went black.

I moaned in pain as my senses started to come back to me. I turned a bit and felt silk move with me, embracing my body. Out of disbelief to what I was feeling, I started to open my eyes, my head throbbing. I nearly had a heart attack when I saw my new surroundings.

I was lying in a king-sized, dark wooden four post bed with see-through plum curtains hung around the frame of the bed. The bed was in the center of the room against the back wall. A matching dresser and furniture pieces were in the room and I couldn't remember the last time I saw anything that nice. I didn't think I ever would see any of these things again, let alone in one piece. As my eyes were scanning the room, there was a sight that spoiled the room. Dean Manson was standing in the doorway, smirking at me.

"Where am I? What happened?" I asked as I tried to sit up, but just stayed down as my head spun.

I didn't dare get out of bed with my pounding head. The new surroundings with the confusion didn't help the headache and stomach turned.

"We are back in New Jersey, in my home... And this is your room for the moment." Manson responded with a matter of fact tone.

I looked at him perplexed.

"How did we get here?" I questioned, narrowing my eyes, my voice sounded distant. "Wait. Did you say for the moment?"

I felt his eyes on me and they weren't just on my eyes anymore. I shuttered. I really was going to be sick.

"You were knocked out so you wouldn't know how we got here, so you can't escape from me." His lips twitched with a smile for a moment. "The bathroom is right there, so please be free to use it before coming down and there are plenty of clothes in the dressers and closet."

With that, Manson left. I made my way into the bathroom, taking staggering steps and keeping near the wall for safety. I couldn't remember the last time I had seen a clean bathroom. I closed the white door behind me and opened the glass door of the shower to start the water. The plumbing worked here? A small smile formed on my lips as I remembered another glass shower.

My fingertips rested on the glass door as my face turned red from the memory. I was giving Sean and Paige a bath in the Pennsylvania home as Aaron came into the room and took a shower despite the fact we were in the room. Knowing his actions would make me uncomfortable, Aaron did it anyway. I didn't turn around to look, but that didn't stop my ears from turning red because he was naked in the same room that I was in.

I took a hot shower for the first time in quite some time. I studied my hands, the nails were short and dirty, so unlike before this whole mess. I grabbed the soap and scrubbed my skin furiously and did the same to my scalp, loathing myself for this whole situation. My skin became red as I tried to rid myself of these feelings. But the water wasn't hot enough to wash away my shame.

When I was done and the water started to cool, I grabbed the fluffy plum towel and went to see what clothes were in the room for me. I slipped on a long black skirt and a white long-sleeve shirt. The clothes didn't fit very well — my new lifestyle trumped any crash diet. But these clothes suited my purpose. I really didn't want him to be looking at me like he had been today. I didn't want that man looking at me in anyway ever again.

I used the brush to work out the zillions of knots in my hair and I left the strands down to dry. It was nice to see my hair down for the first time in such a long time. My hair looked nice in auburn curls, which were almost a surprise after not seeing them in such a long time. I really didn't feel like doing much else, so I went down to try to find where he wanted me to meet him.

I strolled down the polished wood stairs and turned right to find a long table that was completely decked out in table settings. There, at the head of the table, was Dean Manson, appearing clean cut in a full out suit unlike the clothes Aaron and I had been wearing for the last few months. As I stared at the table, I could almost picture Aaron sitting at the table with hands behind his head and feet on the table, his chair slightly rocked back. Aaron's bright, navy blue eyes would be sparkling, burning themselves into my mind as he blasted me with his lopsided grin. The smirk that would tell me he was truly happy and loving life.

"It's nice to see you came to join me." Manson snapped me out of my own little world, bringing me back to the reality he created, not the one I wanted. The reality where Aaron and I were happy, and he had feelings for me.

I sat down next to him on his right-hand side. I played with the soup with my spoon, as he talked to me. Every word that Manson spoke went through one ear and out the other. I didn't eat much—I wasn't used to actual food, especially in real-sized portions. That and being here with Manson totally made food unappetizing. He might as well have been serving Chilled Monkey brains. The home was covered in shadows lending an eerie sense to it. It didn't help that I was sitting next to a man who wanted the guy I cared for to be dead. Manson was also the reason why Ed was dead.

"My girl, is something bothering you?" Manson said.

I didn't look up as I swirled my spoon about in my meal. I taught my brother to never play with his food. Sean would not be happy with me being a hypocrite.

"No, sir," I responded automatically.

"Is there anything wrong with the food?"

"No, sir," I repeated, speaking straight to the point.

"Now, let's get down to business."

I glanced up at Manson, finally peeking up from my cuisine. Dean Manson patted his mouth with his napkin and appeared serious as he locked his eyes on me like a sniper ready for his target.

"You are staying here because you don't want me to go after the others."

Just like a businessman to get to the point. "That's true."

I wished I could have taken in Sean and Paige with me along with the others, but that wasn't part of the deal. I hated myself as I sat there, being taken care of while they were out there starving, using the woods for shelter.

"You are not to run away," Manson continued in a strict tone.

"I figured such as much." My voice still held no emotions.

"You can't help your friends."

I bowed my head low. I held back tears, not wanting show weakness in front of Manson. I could weep the second I got to my room, but not there in front of him.

"Would there be any reason that they would need any help?" I asked.

I had the feeling that Manson was going to go against his word. That or he was fishing for something. Manson grinned.

"No, I guess there wouldn't be." Manson looked at me, interested, he folded his hands on the table before squaring off. "Now there is one more thing we have to discuss."

"And that would be?" My insides gained big black and gray butterflies as he gazed at me that way again. There was graveness in the air. I gulped the nothingness that was my nerves.

"Marriage..."

"What?" I asked as I nearly choked on my water that I was sipping.

"Marriage. You will marry me, so I know you won't go back to that dirt." He spoke in an even tone until the last word as his gray eyes were filled with utter disgust.

"That wasn't part of the deal!" I coughed on the words and tried to stop my voice from squeaking.

Manson was the same age as my father! That was so not right! I would be turning eighteen in another month. I was not ready to get married.

"No, it wasn't part of the deal. Yet, if you have no intention of going against your word, this shouldn't be a problem."

My innards started to die. My stomach felt uneasy.

"Fine, Mr. Manson," I answered with my head bending over again.

"It'll be Dean soon. You can't call your husband by his last name," Manson responded quickly.

I wanted to throw up. Marrying him

made me feel ill. I held back the tears as I put up the hard front. I had to leave before I threw up there on the table. The food sat heavy in my stomach.

"It's been a long day. May I be excused?" My voice was barely over a whisper.

"That's fine. We are to wed in two days."

I stood up, using the table as leverage and staggered up the stairs as calmly as I could. Then rushed into the room and shut the door behind me. My hands shook as I processed what had just happened at dinner. Quickly, I ripped off the clothes he wanted me to wear and chucked them across the room far as possible.

I swayed across the room to the dresser and grabbed one of the plum night gowns. I pushed aside the curtains and curled into the covers, so the material covered my head. It was then that I let out all the tears I'd been holding back. Turning the pillow to my side I hugged the square to my face and chest. I cried myself to sleep as my body shook against the pillow and I thought I was going to be sick. I didn't know if I could handle being with Manson, I really didn't think I could handle that. Ever...

14
Aaron

I woke up feeling empty. I rolled onto my side to hold Lauren against me, but there was only air beside me. I turned onto my other side thinking maybe she would be there. But when I went to put my arm on her, I realized she wasn't there, either. I opened my eyes in panic and sat up to look around at our group. Lauren was nowhere to be seen.

"Lauren? Lauren!" I called out, wishing she would answer me.

I stood up and peered out into the woods around us, but I still didn't find her. Dread seeped through me and an undying fear came over me. What could have happened? Where could she possibly be?

"Lauren!" I yelled out this time, not

caring if I woke the others up.

I ran back to the group to see them stirring. My nerves and heart were freaking out. It felt as if my heart might beat out of my chest. There would have been no reason for Manson to come to our campground and kidnap Lauren and leave the rest of us, right? So where could she be? So many worried eyes stared at me as I fidgeted, attempting to figure out what to do. God, I was calmer when everyone was gone instead of just Lauren.

"Where is Lauren?" Sean asked, rubbing sleep out of his eyes.

Sean stood up, gazing at me. The resemblance between the two became even more noticeable when his sad eyes wouldn't leave mine. Sean's eyes were greenish blue instead of completely blue like Lauren's, but the shape of their eyes was the same. Their hair color was the same, just as the shape of their faces. This was not helping.

"I don't know. Did any of you see her?" I questioned, my eyes scanning each member.

All of them shook their heads as Cole got up, looking around frantically like I had just done. The happiness from the night before seemed to have drained away from me as the alarm and anxiety sank in. That night had been the best of my life. I realized the bliss I felt may never return. I didn't know how to fix the situation, I wanted that cheerfulness back.

"We have to find her!" Cole exclaimed.

I rolled my eyes and faced Cole. Cole expression seemed like a child's and I wondered if I still looked like that. Flashes of what happened to her the last time she was missing came upon me. A pain shot through me as I started to shake a little, trying to understand what could have happened to her. If Lauren had been kidnapped, I would have noticed a harsh struggle since she was in my arms when I went to sleep. I do remember her being in my arms with her head on my chest, so I knew I wasn't imagining that at least.

"No duh, we have to go find her! The problem is trying to think of a plan to get her and figuring out what happened!" I snapped. He couldn't have thought that I wouldn't want to go after her.

Cole just glared at me and I returned the favor. His anger toward me wasn't going to help find Lauren or solve what had happened.

"Did she leave because of you again?" he barked at me as the others went wide eyed.

I was a bit taken aback. I didn't think anyone knew why she left last time. That we had argued about a future together.

"No! We didn't get into an argument last night." I shot back as Lauren's smiles and giggles from our being together flashed before my eyes. "Lauren and I were fine. She was happy with me."

"Did you push her too far? Those kisses were pretty urgent last night." Cole growled his eyes were narrowed balls of fire.

My eyes went wide then thinned at him. I guess he wasn't as asleep as I had thought he was.

"You are always pressuring Lauren to have sex with you. That's why she ran off last time!" Cole wouldn't lower his voice. He continued to yell as I got closer.

Jill jumped between us with a hand at each of our chests to try to separate us even more so as a barrier. "You're bickering isn't going to help us find Lauren. Now shut up and try to act somewhat human instead of like two jackasses!" While screaming at the two us, she moved her head back and forth alternating glances at us.

"What's sex?" Sean whispered to Paige.

She shook her head 'no' in response with a small shrug of her shoulders. I couldn't help but laugh in the middle of all the trouble.

Jill didn't hear them at first, so she looked grumpily at me because of my chuckle.

"Sean, sex is —" Tony started as Jill who appeared like she was going to have a panic attack as she grabbed onto the child and covered his mouth with her dark hand.

"One problem at a time please, people! Okay I get that Lauren isn't here, but that doesn't mean all hell should break loose. Now, let's figure out what we are doing so things can go back to our form of normalcy..." Jill ordered. "And you two act your age."

Jill glared at Cole and I, but you could tell she wasn't ready to lose another one of us. Jill had been close with Mandy and it looked like she wasn't ready to lose Lauren, who'd been taking on the role of the mother of these kids.

I came back from our little argument as I felt someone by my leg and looked down to see Sean. I picked Sean up as he wrapped his arms around my neck to rest his head in the crook of my shoulder. He had grown a little bigger since September. Then, something came to my mind.

"Sean, can I ask you something?" I asked

tenderly.

"Great you are going to bring the kid into this?" Cole sounded frustrated and sighed. He rolled his eyes and dramatically crossed his arms over his chest. I glimpsed back at Sean again, my heartbeat began to speed up.

"Now, Sean, I want you to really remember for me, okay?" I questioned. Sean gazed up at me with sad eyes and nodded his head. "Did that big scary man and Lauren talk yesterday when he had you two?"

Sean's eyebrows went together as he tried to think, and he started to scan around the camp area. "I think they did a little bit… but they were confusing."

This was what I had feared. My nerves began to shake like jumping beans as I thought about what could have gone on in that room.

"Was there any yelling?" I pressed further as he was quiet.

Sean shook his head. "The man wasn't mad, he talked really quietly. He was talking about living with him I think," Sean continued. His head was tilted with his face scrunched up.

I felt the world falling around me at that moment. Part of me knew before Sean had told me. I placed Sean back on the ground as I collapsed Indian style. My breathed deeply, trying to fill my lungs and rid myself of the feeling of being suffocated. I put my face in my hands as my fingers intertwined with my hair. Her jittery behavior now made more sense. Lauren and Manson had possibly talked about her living with him. Lauren was a mess yesterday then I woke up and she was gone.

"God, she'd rather be with an old man than you!" A small laugh came from Cole.

I glared at him. Bolting up, I gripped the front of his shirt as I threw him against a tree before Jill could make a move to stop me. Cole's eyes widened in fear, and I felt someone pulling me back.

"Stop it, you two! We have to get her back before he does something to her!" Her frustration seeped through as she used all her weight to attempt to get me off Cole.

I let go of the worthless piece of garbage in front of me I stared at the ground below my feet.

"He's not going to harm her. He wants me and is using her as bait," I muttered.

"So, let's give him you in exchange for her," commented Cole.

I decided to ignore him as Jill sent

daggers at him with her eyes. Lauren was only with Manson because of me.

"My best bet is that he went back to Jersey, to be more specific, his home in Jersey," I continued as if Cole never spoke.

"Why do you think that?" asked Jill.

"He's been in jail for a while. With the number of followers, he has, even if his house suffered damages, I'm sure he's had it rebuilt. Manson's home probably will look like the disaster never touched his palace." I shook my head, my jaw clenched.

I peeked over at Jill who looked really confused suddenly.

"How do you plan on getting her this time? Walking will take forever."

I shrugged.

"The same as last time, I guess," I said. I hadn't really thought of it. If I rescued her once, it could happen again right?

"Don't you think you getting her last time was a tad on the easy side?" Jill brought up unhurried.

I frowned and tilted my head to comprehend what she was getting at.

"What if... this sounds crazy, but what if he let you get her then?" Jill spoke like she was leading me to an answer she already solved.

I shook my head.

"Let's just get to Lauren. I think I saw some sort of vehicles on the old farm. Hopefully, we can use them and get to Jersey faster."

I started to hike ahead to only take a few moments before the group followed in my footsteps. I picked up Paige and Sean then Jill and Cole picked up the other two so we could run to the farm faster. We needed to get to Lauren soon. In next to no time, the house came into view and we dashed into the barn. I started to look around for something that we could possibly use. There in the corner was a shining jet-black motorcycle with a tan tarp over some of bike to keep dust off.

I moved over it and ripped the tarp off to see the baby. I was practically drooling over the bike as my fingers nervously twitched in desire. I sat on the seat and leaned down as I held the rubber grips, praying that this would work so I could take it. I scanned around for a key and nearly yelped with joy when I saw the last owner was a moron and left the key on a rusted nail on the wall next to the bike. I hoped this baby would work. I put the key in the ignition and turned the handles just to hear the roar of the engine only to turn it off again.

Everyone had their ears covered with their hands.

"What?" I asked innocently I felt like a little kid whose favorite cartoon show was turned into a movie.

Jill was about to say something, but a horse's neigh stopped her. She went to go look out of the barns window to see a couple of horses were headed in our direction.

"I guess some of the animals are returning?" Jill shrugged.

Smiling, I ran to open the barn doors to welcome the tired animals. Two horses galloped in toward a bundle of hay then ate. One horse was brown with a white patch between its deep brown eyes while the other was chalky gray with storm cloud gray speckles all over its body.

I turned to Jill, a plan forming instantly. Probably not the best plan, but it was the only one we had right now.

"You guys will take the horses. Ride them to our hometown, maybe by our old neighborhood to meet up at."

"We'll be meeting you there I take it?" asked Jill with a raised brow.

I turned back to the motorcycle.

"Ooh yeah. Do you guys know how to get there from here?"

"The sun sets in the west and rises in the east, so we head east, and once we're in Jersey, we should know from there. We'll give the horses a bit of a break then head out. Please just meet us there?"

Jill looked scared about to cry from worry mixed with stress. A weak smile formed, and I wrapped my arms around her, forming a brotherly hug. which she returned.

"Jill, I'll get her back and we'll wait for you guys, so don't worry." I squeezed Jill before letting go.

Cole snorted and we stared at him.

"Sure, just leave us." He was challenging me. "Leave us with the responsibility all the time, why don't you? I mean, you left us how many times?"

I stomped up to Cole, narrowing my eyes at him.

"Jill is in charge, so here's your chance to prove to me you're a man. Help her instead of being another person she has to babysit."

"I am a man!" Cole yelled back at me furiously, as if his voice could kill me.

"A man isn't told by age, but by his

actions," I whispered Ed's words to him as I took long strides over to the motorcycle.

Again, I turned the key and rode off out of the barn to watch a teary Jill, Paige, and Sean behind me as I went east on my quest for Lauren. The wind whipped past me as the engine roared, making me feel free like I had once felt, but then I remembered why I was even heading in this direction. I had to get to Lauren and live to tell the tale.

I left the motorcycle a few blocks away from Manson's home. The house seemed to be lifeless. Everything appeared dark until I reached the back of the house. A speck of light flickered up by a window on the second story. I glanced around and didn't see anyone, so I pulled myself up a tree near the house.

Finally, I worked myself to the branch to level with the window. A candle was shrinking on a small holder. The flames danced around the big room. Every shape of the furniture and the dark wood reflected the light back to its source. My eyes scanned over every part of that room and saw a bed in the middle of the room until they stopped on the bulge in the middle of the bed.

And just as if the lump heard my heart's desire, the figure stretched itself and rolled over onto the other side so that it faced me. Lauren's dark eyelashes created long shadows on her thinning cheeks and the curve of the lashes and cheek bones collided.

I stared at the ground below me as I realized Lauren was being well taken care of, no thanks to me. I sighed, recognizing maybe I should leave her there with Manson. I began to climb down the tree after I noticed that Lauren was safe and sound, better than I could ever do for her. That was when the candle flickered as the door opened on the opposite side of the room, Dean Manson walked into her room. I watched through her window with anger and repulsion came over me. I couldn't stop what was happening, but the scene was getting to me. My whole body was rigid; my grip on the tree branch was tense.

Manson walked closer to Lauren just so he could rest his hand on her head. He ran one of his fingers through her curly hair as the light caught every twist and turn of her locks. My heart ached as I watch him touch her like I wanted to, like I had done. I took a deep breath, hoping the painful twinge would just go away when I saw his lips press against her forehead. I wanted to rip that man limb by limb. I was going to get her out of there if it was the last thing I'd ever do.

15

Lauren

Soreness overcame me the next morning when I woke up. My eyes and throat burned from crying myself to sleep and my limbs cried out in tenderness from sleeping in a tight ball. The silk sheets felt like grime to my skin and I felt ashamed of myself for getting in this situation.

I nearly jumped a foot in the air as the door opened. There stood a man you feared yet admired for his strength as he destroyed you.

"You must now get up and meet me for breakfast. Don't wear the clothes you wore to dinner. There are much more than that." No good morning or anything, just right to the point.

Manson left me alone and I took a few

minutes to get out of bed to get ready. My body was refusing to move correctly. I grabbed a shirt and bottoms, not really paying attention to what I was taking out of the drawers and then I went into the bathroom to get ready. My eyes widened after I put the shirt on. I looked down to where my hands stopped. The shirt didn't even cover my midsection.

I threw on the long jeans that rested low on the hips. This outfit was not going out of the room to be seen by a middle age man and his weirdo followers. Shuffling through the drawers I noticed there seemed to be a trend with the clothes, not much fabric. I glanced again in the mirror not believing the image in front of me. This thin shadow of what I use to be, it made me nauseous.

I opened my bedroom door to find a guy standing guard, which made me uneasy. The thought that someone would always have an eye on me caused a shudder to shoot up my spine. I attempted to stroll swiftly away from the guy and not seem like I was up to anything. I rushed down the stairs with my arms around my middle. My arms were a poor effort to cover myself. I found Dean Manson sitting at the table waiting for me. With slow steps, I made my way to the table, restraining the urge to play with my hair, a nervous habit, as I kept my arms concealing the exposed skin.

Dean Manson stood up and pulled out the chair next to him so I could sit down. My insides were fluttering. I didn't want to be near him. I wanted Aaron's arms around me instead Manson's. He pushed my seat in as I stared down at the tablecloth. I felt a slight pressure on my head. Even though I couldn't see what he had done, I knew Dean Manson had kissed the top of my head. I wanted to vomit and to scrub every inch of me.

He sat down, grinning at me as the gloom just seeped through me. I couldn't even fake a smile, so I kept my eyes glued to the table, and then a plate of food was placed there. Manson started to talk to me, and I just kept nodding my head like I was paying attention, though my ears seemed to be turned off.

"A bit distracted, are we?"

I just looked up at the adult in front of me. "Sorry." My voice was monotone. I just pushed around the food on my plate, "I'm not hungry that's all."

"You know, the wedding is tomorrow."

I just nodded my head, yes. I was unable

to speak.

"I knew you wouldn't be leaping for joy over this… arrangement, but I thought I would get a little more life out of you."

I just stared blankly at him and started to fear what he meant by that as I felt a draft on my ribs. I so didn't want that man touching me. I held back a quiver at how repulsed I was.

I was leaning more to one side to get a little farther from him.

"Now, Lauren, I've been planning our wedding tomorrow, so you don't have to worry about any of the details."

I just nodded my head. I didn't want to marry this guy and I so didn't want to be doing any part of the planning of my forced marriage.

"Now, what will you be doing today?"

I wanted to roll my eyes at that comment. I was practically being blackmailed to stay with Dean Manson to protect the guy I loved, and he was asking me how I planned on spending my day. There wasn't really anyone or anything to keep me busy since the asteroids. My new family was God knows where with the guy I'd much rather be with. Then to top it off, I apparently had prison guards.

"I'll probably go back to my room after

taking a book from the library," I responded with a shrug, not sure if I would be able to even see the letters without my glasses.

I took one bite of the breakfast and decided I was going to throw up if I had to eat near Manson. His façade was obviously fake, and I was insulted he thought I was dumb enough to fall for it. Aaron told me what a horrible man Manson was, and watching him carry out this act was nauseating.

"That sounds nice. I'll see you for dinner. Also, make sure the white dress in your room fits you. Remember, this is your last night in that room since tomorrow night, you'll be in my room."

Dean Manson just loved to just share the good news. It was one good thing right after another with him. After he left, I attempted to eat little of the food, but someone came into the room and took the plate away from me. With a sigh, I watched my breakfast be carried away from me, so I decided to go upstairs to see how much I should worry about this dress he had already had for the wedding. How did Dean Manson even get the dress?

Taking many deep breaths, I prayed not to find a hooker wedding dress in the closet.

After all, I'd seen my everyday outfits. As I neared the room, I saw the man still standing in front of my door. The guard's face was stone cold, staring straight ahead as I rushed into the room and closed it quickly.

With a racing heart, I went to the closet thinking this was so not how I thought my wedding would be. Opening the closet's French doors, I found the hanger that was in a bag with the logo of what was once the local wedding shop printed on the back. Without breathing, I took the bag out of the closet. I placed the bag on my bed. Leaning over, I took the dress out. It felt the air being sucked out of my lungs. I stared at the dress. Nervously, I exchanged my current sorry excuse for clothing with what was supposed to be my wedding dress.

I zipped the back of the dress up and tied the halter by the back of my neck. I noticed there was a mirror in the corner. My hair was a bit of a mess, so I tied my hair in a bun using the hair brush on the dresser. There were a few pieces jewelry in a dark wooden, highly detailed box. I grabbed a pair of dangle earrings that were tear drop stones to try on for when I glimpsed into the mirror once more to see if that had helped any.

I was in a sleek white dress that sparkled lightly in the light that came through my window. I turned to my side to see a small train of fabric behind me. A little longer then it probably should be, but halter helped a little. So, the dress didn't fit me perfectly, but overall, wasn't too bad.

I curled up in bed to read comfortably after finding more comfortable clothes. I became part of the world that I was reading about, forgetting that time was passing by as I read each word. It started to get harder to read and I was about to light a candle when it clicked that I was in serious trouble.

I threw down the book on my bed and jumped off, not caring about saving my spot in my book. I ran through the door, I heard it crash behind me as I ran down the stairs two at a time. My heart raced as I wondered how much trouble I was in.

I was late for dinner and I had no idea how he was going to react. When I got down there, the table was empty and dark. My heart was racing, as I tried to figure out if I was early or late. It was a serious, horrible surprise. I screamed when I felt someone take hold of my shoulders and whip me around. Manson was standing in front of me, glaring down upon me as his fingers left marks on my shoulders. Terror overcame me, as my breathing became labored and I started to wonder if killing me was too low for him to do.

"I'm… sorry… I was reading… and lost track of time." I stammered. My tongue was almost tripping over the words.

My eyes were big with worry as I tried to force some air into my lungs. Manson didn't say a word as he dragged me up the stairs with a tighter grip on my arm. I wouldn't allow myself to whimper in pain in front of him, but with my voice was drenched in pure fear, as I apologized over and over. Bruises were already forming on my skin.

The sorrys didn't seem to wear Dean Manson down at all as he tossed me into my room. I almost lost my footing as I grabbed onto a bedpost. Holding onto the wood for dear life, I feared he would come after me again, but instead, he slammed the door. A soft click followed. He had locked me in. Shaking, I fell to the floor into fetal position with tears just waiting to be released.

I was lying on my side, facing the door, too afraid to fall asleep. If that was a preview of what was to come, I wanted out! I'd go live in a cave if I had to just as long as I didn't have to be near him. It wasn't like anyone knew where my family was anyway. So, they would be safe, and I wouldn't be with Manson.

"Pst!"

A noise made me sit up and I turned to face the window. I jumped out of bed and quietly rushed to the window to see Aaron sitting in a tree, looking a little odd as he gazed into my room. Aaron looked straight from a movie of a crazy person staring into my room.

"Aaron?" I asked, squinting into the dark world to look at what I thought was the very male I was protecting.

The image before me grinned as he nodded. Aaron inched himself closer to the window, making me worry as he was on the weaker side of the branch, until he was able to reach over to the windowsill. I gasped when he fell from the branch to hang on the sill. Together, we got him in. My skin met his, tangible proof I was not losing my mind.

The air seemed to be stuck in my lungs as I got lost in Aaron's eyes. With shaky hands, I hesitantly reached out for his face. Tenderly, I held it between my two hands, closing the space between us. Once I knew he was real, I wrapped my arms tightly around his neck, afraid that he would leave me if I didn't. I didn't care how dirty or how much he smelled. I buried my face into his neck, never wanting him to leave me.

"You smell and look nice," he whispered in my ear, which sent shivers down my spine. "Why did you leave?" Aaron sounded wounded and baffled.

I closed my eyes firmly, not wanting to explain the horrible situation to Aaron.

"For you..." I spoke softly.

Aaron pulled away a little to look at me in confusion. I took a deep breath and glanced out the window, afraid that I might breakdown before I got the whole story out.

"I traded me for you. If I stay with Manson, he's going to stop chasing after you and the rest of the group."

"You..." He paused. "You turned yourself in to him to get him off me?"

I just nodded.

"Are you nuts?" Aaron nearly shrieked.

I rolled my eyes and shook my head as he started to pace around the room. I could hear his voice was sopping in shocked frustration as he tried to keep his voice down.

"Aaron—"

"You can't honestly think he's going to keep to his word!"

I couldn't read Aaron's face. I walked over to him and snatched his hand, pulling him over to me. I held his face so I could talk to him and I smiled feeling as if Aaron were acting like a kid. Aaron looked worried, frazzled, and irritated.

"Lauren, I don't think he's going to keep to his word…" Aaron appeared rather beaten by that and I glimpsed down. I wrapped my arms around his chest to rest my head on his shoulder. Affectionately, yet protectively, his arms went around my shoulders.

"Figured, but it was worth trying," was all I could mutter.

Aaron bent over to reunite our lips, but the twist of the key came to our attention as I dashed Aaron into the closet and closed the door in his face. Nearly tripping over my feet, I ran to my bed. The door started to open as I jumped into bed, but before I could get under the sheets,

Manson was standing in my doorway. I was out of breath, hoping he wouldn't notice, and I was actually thanking God that he didn't use his lights to save his power.

"I want to apologize for my behavior earlier this evening. I thought you were plotting to escape," Manson paused and I tried to slow my heartbeat. "Well, I just thought you went back to a certain creature."

"I was here reading," I spoke slowly, restraining myself from gazing at the door.

Manson was no longer looking at my face as we talked. The moon light shined in the room, giving me just enough light to see where his eyes had travelled. My face must have turned bright red, which I was again happy for the darkness, as I moved my legs under the sheets, wishing that I had my smiling frog pajamas instead of this pathetic excuse of a nightgown Manson gave me. He cleared his throat and started to head out the door.

"Now get a good night's rest for tomorrow. It's a big day for us. After all, it's not every day you marry the soon-to-be ruler of the world."

I nodded my head, feeling my mouth dry up from dread. Aaron was really pushing things by being there. With a simple nod of Manson's head and a smile, he left. With a big sigh, I fell back on my bed, trying to relax and figure out everything that had been going on.

"You're marrying Manson!" I just closed my eyes as Aaron whisper-yelled when the closet door swung open.

I just rolled over on my side, throwing my sheets over my head, making sure I was completely covered. I pulled my knees into my chest yearning for a pair of ruby red slippers so I could just wish myself back home. I felt the bed sag next to me, but I didn't move.

"God, I forgot what a bed felt like, not even just that mattress we were on in the apartment, but a real bed."

I grinned at Aaron's comment, but bit down on my lip to stop the small laugh that wanted to be let free. The bed sunk a little more right beside me as an arm moved me close to a chest. Still, I wouldn't come out of the sheets.

"Why are you marrying him?"

I cringed. Yet he sounded childish and angry at that.

"I mean I just brought up the conversation of having children in the future and you bit my head off." Aaron continued.

I rolled my eyes, then sat up after I ripped the sheets off my head. I glared down at Aaron. He seemed too comfortable on the bed in the house of a man who wanted him dead.

"I don't want to marry him. It wasn't part of the original agreement, but if I don't, I'm afraid he might go back against his word and try to kill you."

Aaron sat up; his eyes seemed more understanding now. "Lauren, what have I been saying about not taking on the world all by yourself?"

I sighed and rolled my eyes. I was getting sick of sighing too.

"I know, but I figured it was worth the shot. When he had me and Sean back in Pennsylvania, it really hit me how much he knew about us and what was at stake. I had to solve some of the problems, at least attempt to save all of our lives."

We were staring into each other's eyes and he brushed a strand of hair behind my ear.

"You probably should go before someone finds you. He has a man who stands guard in front of my door and the whole point of me being here is to keep you safe," I whispered.

"Don't worry I'll find a way to help you

escape tomorrow."

Wasn't he listening to anything I had been saying?

"Aaron, no, you're supposed to be protecting Sean and staying far from here. I'm entrusting my only living relative, my little brother, with you."

"Your brother is safe with Cole and Jill; they are meeting us here—"

I was pissed now. That was probably not even strong to describe my emotions at that moment.

"That defeats the whole reason of me being with Manson. You need to get out of here with the others. That's an order!"

"Not without you!"

"Yes! You—"

I stood up, anticipating Aaron would follow me. Yet he took hold of my arm, stopping me from going any farther, leaving me glaring at him.

"I'm not leaving you in that man's hands. There is no way I can live the rest of my life knowing that I'm leaving you to be forced to accept him touching you and…" He groaned. "I can't even think about it!" He growled with fire in his eyes.

"If I go against our agreement—" Before I could utter another word, Aaron covered my lips with his, then darted out of the window before anything else could be said.

Aaron left so he couldn't be argued with. I could hit him. I loved him…

Getting ready for the wedding made me miss my family so much. I mean parents or at least the ones that love you should be at your wedding. If not your love ones, at least a man who loved you should be at the end of the aisle and I didn't have any of that. I pushed the earrings through each hole, making the tears on them swing. My hair was in a neat, tidy bun with one strand curly and loose to hang on the side of my face. I nervously straightened the dress in front of a mirror as I thought of the dress I wanted to get for prom. My mom and I were ahead of the game, building up enthusiasm even though school hadn't even started.

A faint smile started to play on my lips as my imagination got the best of me. Aaron was standing behind me in a tux, groomed and suave with a smirk on his face. I grinned but soon vanished as I remembered Aaron wasn't there.

A thunderous knock sounded on the door. Before I could reply, the door swung open to show the bodyguard there. I knew that it was time for the wedding.

Bowing my head low, I followed the man down the stairs to the backyard without glancing around me. My heart felt heavy with sorrow, but I finally looked up after walking through the back door. Standing there were a few of his followers and standing in the middle up ahead was Dean Manson in black dress pants and a white dress shirt positioned with ridged military posture.

My heart felt as if it had it hit an iceberg, sinking down into my stomach without any sign of being saved. Even though the days were growing warmer, I felt cold and wobbly.

The people there stared blankly at me, shells of what used to be human, and I felt my legs could give out at any moment from nerves. Yet I took a step forward, feeling the small train being pulled slightly, as if the grass was attempting to hold me back. Repeating the words, *'I so didn't want this life'* in my head. My stomach ached from nerves and my mouth dried up. It wouldn't surprise me if I had been trembling.

I wanted to cry as I finally reached the front. As the man marrying us spoke, I couldn't concentrate even though it was my wedding, and I should have been fully focused. It wasn't worth it. What was the point? I came back to earth though when he asked if I took Dean Manson as my husband.

I was about to open my mouth, gazing into those stormy eyes and knowing there was only one answer I could give. If I didn't give that one answer, the whole agreement would be over. So much was riding on those two simple words. With all those people there, I could have been easily killed without them really moving or having to use much effort. I knew they were dangerous and there wasn't anyone to stop them from killing me then my family.

"I—"

"She doesn't, nor will she ever!" A yell cut me off from answering.

With my mouth wide open, I turned my head to find where that voice came from, completely shocked at what I was staring at.

16
Aaron

Standing there I had no idea what I was doing. I didn't have a plan or anything and I wouldn't call the piece of a metal light post I had in my hand a plan. It was just on the ground, and I thought it could at least provide some sort of aid. I probably should've formed a plan first. Especially since I was about to march into hostile territory. People feared and yet followed Manson. He had weapons unlike everyone else, if Ed had been right, and I had no one to stop him or his followers from exterminating me. Yet there I stood with only a metal rod in my hand, staring at Dean Manson with no idea of what to do next.

The long, green grass swallow up the edge of Lauren's dress as her eyes widened to their limits. She kept turning her head to watch Dean Manson and me. I was sure she was waiting for the first move. Lauren's hands twisted nervously while she bit her lips. Yet while Lauren seemed to be on edge, Manson's smirk didn't go unnoticed.

"I knew you would come." Manson's voice was smooth.

Manson pulled Lauren into his chest, which made her gasp as she fell clumsily into him. Lauren's worried appearance just grew as his arm wrapped around her middle, making her appear fragile pressed against that thick man.

"I knew taking her would draw you in. It's like killing two birds with one stone. I get to kill you and get have a lovely new, young wife to replace the one that left me while I was in prison because of you. It's just an added bonus that I get to watch you suffer. Vengeance is a beautiful thing, boy."

A chunky finger from his other hand glided over her jaw in a slow gentle stroke to tease me, not to be a comfort to her. Gripping the metal tighter, I made indents in my hand and I wished that I could do the same to Manson's head. A grand grin formed on his face little by little.

"It's the end of the line for you, Aaron. Kill him." Manson shouted with a laugh.

The few followers Manson had there came at me. I really didn't like the numbers in the fight. The supporters materialized from nowhere all as majestic as Manson himself. They crept up to me like animals hunting their pray, hoping that they could please their master and give him the prize. Okay so twenty against one was definitely not looking good. Manson sat down bringing Lauren with him in his lap. He appeared so possessive over her it just fueled anger.

As one went to hit me in the face, I backed up against another one. I struggled against their grasp, only to realize I was pathetic for not lasting long enough to save her and myself. Being held captive by a man with a stone grip, a woman got the opportunity to punch me in the left eye, making the world to go black. The real world came back to me one dot at a time. Unfortunately, the vision wouldn't stay as a hard object was driven into my stomach. An ear-piercing yell in the distance made me know there was much more to endure. Biting down on my tongue to stop myself from screaming out, my face got in the way of another fist.

The man who had been holding me tossed me to the ground. Before I could get up to defend myself or at least attempt to use the metal object I had brought, the object was used on me. Feeling the metal strike my side hard, I bit down on my tongue. The group, working together, started to attack me, kicking me as if they were fighting for a soccer ball caught in the middle and even though it was pointless to try to get the ball in that manner, you kick rock-hard anyway. Hearing and feeling my insides blaring at my stupidity, I realized that at least a couple of ribs had cracked. I tried to bring my knees in to protect my remaining ribs, but before I could, I let out a yell as the metal collided with my forehead.

The world around me went black and swirled in and out. Warm and thick, a liquid that smelled of copper crawled down my face, falling into the crevice of my eye. Blood continued slipping down my face as I was lifted off the ground. My body throbbed all over, and I wasn't sure what was happening or whether or not I would make it out of there with Lauren or even alive. My thoughts were interrupted as my body was dropped onto the ground, a groan escaping from my lips. I wasn't able to hold back anymore. I was fighting to stay conscious.

"You guys may go into the house. I'll take the rest of the matters into my own hands," Manson said.

"You're a monster!" Lauren's voice sounded horrified, furious, and anguished, and I felt her kneel next to me.

"He never told you what happened that night I was arrested, did he?" Manson's voice was still unruffled as if he didn't hear what Lauren had said.

I wasn't sure if it was because blood was sinking into my stomach or because of the guilt, but I felt sick. Lauren touched my cheek. Her caress was gentle and understanding, as if his words never touched her ears.

"It doesn't matter." Lauren's words were soft on my ears.

"Oh, I know women too well and I know you're curious. You want to believe Aaron is who he pretends to be."

"Aaron has only been himself!" Lauren snapped; her hands were still on my face.

The embarrassment of that night made me turn to my side to spit up blood, it wasn't a lot, but I still heaved up the liquid none the less.

I came to save Lauren, not make her suffer more by watching me die. I so didn't want to work so hard for the rescue to only ruin it by a mistake I made a couple of years ago. I promised myself I wouldn't do anything like that again. Yet, I knew she had a right to know and I had put it off for many months…

"With your last breath, Aaron, I want you to tell her the truth. I only know part of it myself. After all, it was because of that night that I had to spend those years in prison."

I tried to open my eyes. One was swollen from when the girl smacked me while the other had dried blood crusting over it.

"You promised you wouldn't hurt him I if I stayed with you!"

I could tell in Lauren's tone she knew that was a lame excuse, but she was desperate, we both were. Through slits, I could see her just staring down at me for dear life. With enormous effort I took a deep breath. The new breath made me wince as it felt like knives stabbing my insides.

"That night, my friends and I —"

"Aaron, please just save your breath!" Lauren pleaded as she interrupted me.

"Don't waste yours, Lauren, for telling

this story is going to be the last thing he does, before I get the pleasure of finishing off this nobody." Manson snapped at her.

I grimaced as Lauren's shaky hand glided into mine, and even through the throbbing, I grabbed onto hers. I wanted to feel something other than pain. I interlaced our fingers possibly for the last time.

"I wasn't quite sure what my friends were planning, and I didn't really care. I had gotten into a pretty bad argument with my dad, which really made my mom upset. Horrible words were said, and I regret them now." I paused as I wrapped my free arm around my chest feeling my rib ripple in tenderness. "One of my friends at the time started driving, the music was loud as the windows were wide open. Before we pulled up in front of a house."

My heart put in extra work to keep my body working under all the stinging pain and embarrassment of my foolishness from a couple of years ago. I closed my eyes, my ribs sensitive with each breath I struggled to take.

"He was part of a ring of dealers, got to love drugs roots in small towns. There were older guys who made deals with high schoolers to get to the younger crowd. My friend brought us along because it was a bigger shipment to pick up and they needed more recruits. We got into the house, since it was dark, it was hard to see everyone. But I could tell they were there. I felt all their eyes on us. My friend shook hands with this one big guy, who then shook me. Then he started talking about what he wanted me to do, and I just couldn't take it, so I ran."

I closed my eyes and took a straining couple of breaths.

"Just as I was rounding the corner, I saw a couple cops cars blaring toward the house. I ran away down the street, my heart thumping in my ears. That's why I always felt bad about running out on you guys," I took a moment to stop as my body ached and I wondered if I would finish this story without dying. "I ran out on my friends when they needed me before and I knew I was doing the same to you. It just brought back bad memories. The cops saw me and started chasing me. My friends got arrested that night, and some of the bigger dealers.

"I kept running until I came across an old warehouse, I thought it had been abandoned for years. I climbed on the old dumpster to go through the broken window. While I was hiding in there, I heard some voices. Then I saw a couple lights were on the other side of the place. Getting closer I saw a few guys standing together. Manson was one of them, and he was talking about getting rough with some politician. He was going to put the guy in the hospital just so a few regulations got passed.

"The cops came in and busted Manson. Even though they had been searching for me, they took him. One cop though found me and gave me the choice, either they'll take me or…" I paused as I stared into Lauren's eyes. "If I testified against not only the dealers, but also Manson, I was off the hook."

Absentmindedly, my thumb traveled over hers while I told my little tale. A deep chest laugh came through quietly until it was loud as thunder. My eyes clamped down as the injuries' aftermath radiated through my body. If I had not been holding Lauren's hand, I might have welcomed death.

"How adorable. Too bad you will have to die now, Aaron, and I get to keep her."

Leaning my head flat on the ground as I took shallow breaths, a thought ran through my mind. A small smile formed on my lips making a few cuts reopen.

"You're about to die and you're

laughing?" Dean Manson asked slowly.

"Yes."

In the brief time I had spent with Ed, he had as much of an impact on my life as my adoptive dad. I laid there, hoping that the two men were both looking down at me at that moment grinning with pride. In Ed's case it might be looking up at me, but cheerful none the less in his bizarre way.

"I'm not afraid of you." I chuckled, feeling a little blood dripping out of my mouth.

That's what high school teaches you, others made you fear them for power and their lack of security. School trained you how to deal with people.

"That doesn't matter to me because you're going to die."

"You're not a man," I spat out, trying to control my breathing to feel fewer twinging nerves.

Ed's face was fresh in my mind as he spoke to me in a hurry, yet his words had meant a lot to me. I was making my death less enjoyable for Manson. If I was to die right here and now, I was going to destroy his dream of seeing me die under his power.

"I'm close to twice your age, and you're

saying, you're more of a man than I am?" I could hear Dean Manson give another deadly snort, he was being selective with his listening.

"You shot a man in cold blood as he risked his own life for seven strangers. He took all of those kids in even though one was very sick, and another was being hunted down. He died protecting us from you, but before he died, he shared some wisdom with me. A man isn't defined by age, but by his actions." I tried to peek at Lauren, wondering if she thought I was being a man or just a stupid boy.

Even as that thought came through my mind, I knew it was ridiculous, but I was still curious if she understood that I did what I was doing for her. That everything I had done in the past months was because of her. She really meant the world to me and I would do anything for her.

"What a bunch of nonsense!" Dean Manson voice became loud and gruff.

"It isn't nonsense!" Lauren shouted, sounding furious.

Her warm body pressed close to my chest and an arm wrapped around me. I ignored the tenderness, wishing I could put my arms around her in return.

"I love you and—" I started.

"Oh, stop this nonsense!" Manson roared to stop me from talking more.

I glanced over at Manson who was standing tall and livid. He moved his hand to behind him to take out something slowly. I started to sit up to try and push Lauren to the side as the gun came into view. My body throbbed as I stood up. I didn't care about me; I was done for anyway. Manson pointed the gun straight at my chest, probably the same gun he used on Ed. The click of the gun echoed through my ears as my world went into slow motion.

Lauren tried to push me out of the way of the bullet. Grabbing onto her, I turned us around just in time. I cringed over her shoulder and she screamed. Falling to the ground, sensing something warm and sticky seeping through the shoulder of the back of my shirt, I smiled.

"Missed my heart," I whispered to Lauren as she collapsed with me.

Tears streamed down her face as she tried to catch me from collapsing on the ground. I lay down slowly on the grass as a little sunlight shined down on us. The back of the leather coat grew moist as my blood seeped out from the wound. I couldn't believe I was dying. Yet a small smirk formed on my lips.

"Hey, look at me," I held her hand as she leaned near to me, "Despite what we've been through, I'd do it again just to keep every last moment with you. There isn't a single thing I wouldn't do for you, I love you…"

The other night of us dancing came back to me. The words of that song finally sank into me. The love songs finally made sense. I used to not comprehend what the lyrics meant. People just say how romantic they were and stuff, then there I was actually dying as if I were part of the song, living the song. I gazed into her blue eyes as tears were building up and falling down her sad face.

"This is all my fault, Aaron," Lauren muttered, closing her eyes for a moment.

"I have one tiny trick up my sleeve," I spoke to her in a hushed tone, Lauren raised an eyebrow, yet I could see more agony in her eyes then curiosity.

Gently urging Lauren off me, I pressed myself up griping the cool metal around my bloody fingers that was left carelessly beside me after being used against me. Standing up, I used the metal to get myself up. Manson was watching furiously, and I aimed to act like him, strived to be unreadable.

"Can't you just die already?" Dean Manson just asked causally.

I smiled at the stubborn man in front of me, who I realized was just as willful as me. The strain felt horrible as my breath came hard and laborious. I nearly struggled to stop myself from hunching over. If I was going to die, I wanted to die in peace knowing that he was dead and couldn't hurt the others or Lauren.

"Look at yourself. Just lie down and die. You're just making this harder on yourself— making your death so much more fun for me, but worse for Lauren."

I didn't have to look at her, but I knew Manson's words were true. Yet, I had to do make one last attempt. Feeling the metal digging into my hand, I felt calmer than ever. Lauren glided as if in the clouds, foggy minded and went over to Manson, just to drift her fingers along his face, dragging him toward her. It felt like the bullet had hit my heart as I saw her slide his face toward her.

Hesitantly, her lips met his. Seeing Manson wrap his arms around her to mesh his vulgar lips against hers, I realized what Lauren was doing. Securing an arm tightly so his grip was firm on her hip, Manson's voice started as he kept his eyes glued on my girl that was forced alongside him.

"Is this a nice little pathetic attempt of begging for his life? There will be plenty of time for that, dear, and much more." He turned to look at me, but it was too late. Using the last bit of my strength, I pushed the metal into his abdomen.

Two screams filled the air when there was just a tiny bit of the metal sticking out of Manson. He choked on blood as he pushed Lauren into me. We hit the ground together. She crawled closer to me as Goliath went down, bleeding to his death. I tried harder to glance at Lauren again as she sat over me, struggling to turn me over.

"Let me get a look at the wound." She shook slightly bent over.

Grimacing, I tried to turn toward her. I wanted to scream as Lauren tried to take the jacket off, but we were interrupted.

"My... followers will not be... pleased to see... you still here with me here like... this." He laughed through gurgles of blood.

Lauren put an arm around me to help me up. Biting the inside of my mouth as we limped our way away from there, I heard Manson calling to his followers. Lauren shook in fear. I heard him order his minions to find us, while telling some to help him. With every order, his voice grew quieter, less majestic. I kept feeling like I was fading out, just like him.

Rain began to pour down on us as clouds started to roll in while we wondered how we would escape at the rate we were moving. I questioned who was falling over more, Lauren or me. Finally, we buckled down by some weeds by a lake, which might had been the very same one we began our journey at. I closed my eyes as I lay down on the cool grass. The air became heavy, harder for me to breathe in. I felt Lauren fall next to me with an arm around me.

"I want you to keep an eye out. I told the others to come here and they'll be on horses..." I struggled to talk.

I felt like I was about to lose consciousness. I turned to glance at Lauren, seeing her bend over me. There was a rip and blood pouring out of her side. I felt guilty realizing that I must have gotten her with the metal a little when I stabbed Manson. Lauren's eyes showed tenderness as she looked at me; then she wiped her lips, which made me smile, she hated kissing him. Rain mixed with tears dripped down her face.

"Don't cry. It's going to be okay because I love you and would do anything for you no matter what," her eyes filled in tears as she bent down to me while my voice sounded hoarse.

"Please don't talk like you're dying!" Lauren pleaded.

I pulled her closer to me, so her lips were near mine. I wanted to be with her longer and I was being forced to leave her again. Unlike the other times I left her though, I wouldn't be coming back. I wouldn't be getting a welcome back hug like I had received in Pennsylvania. I loved her too much to leave her like that. Staring into her eyes, everything we went through ran through my mind.

Delicately, I touched her lips to mine for just a short moment, a whisper of a contact, but Lauren didn't leave. This left me to say my parting words against her lips. My eyes closed as my mind stared to drift away. Feeling began to leave my body and I was only able to sense a slight tinge of warmth from her lips against mine.

"Falling in love with you was unexpected but risking my life for you was the easiest thing

I've ever done. Even in death I won't stop protecting you…"

Epilogue

The air was different and clean after the rain shower as the breeze flowed into the house. The world was fresh and ready to start off new, a clean slate for the world. We needed that new beginning after everything we went through. I felt that we at least deserved that much.

What was supposed to be another school year turned out so much differently than I ever could have imagined. Although we paid a dear price for survival and lost many things, we still weren't ready to face, it had been the most interesting year of my life. Heart-wrenching and painful, but also inspiring and beautiful.

I limped inside the house and began to head back to the bedroom I shared with Paige and Sean. After everything that had happened, they wanted to stay close to everyone. The two still didn't trust Tony and Kyle with their tricks. I couldn't really blame Sean and Paige though, and I was happy to have them close by. After I fell unconscious, Jill and Cole came with the group, finding us where we were to take us back to the home in Pennsylvania. I still don't know how they found the place again.

All I remember though was waking up back in the house, not believing I was alive — in pain, lots of agony — but none the less alive, which kind of made the throbbing welcoming. Watching the little ones sleeping brought back those memories.

"It still hasn't sunk in, has it?" A gentle whisper tickled my ears as her arms encircled my chest in the smallest touch, knowing I was still in pain.

Nuzzling against the top of Lauren's head, I put an arm around her with the other against the wall, still feeling unstable on my own two feet.

"No, I can't believe I'm alive," I responded in a low voice.

"Just be happy Jill has seen too many medical television shows."

I gave a small chuckle, which made me grimace — my ribs were still sore. I sighed, then took a shallow breath.

I intertwined her fingers with mine then

let our hands fall to our sides as we watched Paige and Sean sleeping and cuddling with the stuffed animals, they found the first time we came through here. Since this had been the first place, we felt comfortable after the asteroids hit, we thought it was only fitting we made it our new home.

"Hey, you couldn't get rid of me that easily. It's going to take a lot more than a beating and being shot for you to lose me. I love you too much to be able to get written off."

A smile formed on her lips and her eyes twinkled. "Who says that's a bad thing?" She gazed up at me, her chin resting against my chest.

I gave a short snort. "You're stuck with me until the world falls to pieces, and if we're not still standing, we'll still find a way to be together."

Now continue the *End of the Line* series with *Going Rogue*. *Going Rogue* is the novella of when the group was in the town and Aaron leaves them all those months. Where did he go? What did he go through? What made him return?

Going Rogue

1
Aaron

My heart pounded against my chest as I bolted down the stairs. Screams rose from the rooms that I passed then a thud as someone was thrown into the hall. Jumping over the body I made my way down the stairs not even checking to see if that person was okay. I needed air as my throat was closing in. Shoving the broken door of the building I was once again outside. My head was spinning and the shouts from my surroundings were only mixing with my own inner arguments. What was I doing? I shouldn't have put Lauren in that kind of situation. Pinning her to the mattress like that was dumb and we weren't alone. God forbid if we started something and the relationship went bad how were we suppose to make things work out with an ex? We could potentially get to a point where we hated each other. Yet, I doubted we could survive without each other. Our numbers have been helpful.

Or things could work out between us…

Racking my fingers through my hair I took deep breaths, my steps slowed slightly. A day away from them should be fine. Just enough time to clear my head then go back to them so that we can be one big happy group. I'm probably just overanalyzing the situation. Me desiring to be close to Lauren was probably because we were stuck together for so long with no one else around. That had to be it because there was a lack of options. Finally sitting down I glanced around not fully sure where I had wandered off to. It was quiet. I couldn't even hear the town. I had traveled a good enough distance that even the noise wouldn't travel.

I stared up at the sky. Dark clouds were rolling in. When was the last time it had rained?

Yet, all I could see were two blue eyes staring at me. Those blue eyes were still on me, confused by me being on top of her. I really wanted to kiss those lips once again. We had kissed one other time, but it was quick, chaste, this time, would've been the real deal. Would her lips be soft? Though the bigger question was, would she return the gesture?

She hadn't pushed me off of her…

Laying down I rested my head down on some moss. I just stared up above unable to close my eyes.

A shuffle of leaves woke me causing me to sit up quickly. It had gotten darker and I started to wonder how long I had been passed out. There was movement to the left of me and I slowly got up, but kept myself crouched behind some trees. Keeping myself fleshed against the tree I peeked around to see what it was. My heart pounded in my chest when I saw a light. The flashlight went from one side to another. Squinting I tried to make out who was holding the light.

"How far of a search does Manson have for the boy?"

"Last I heard I heard New Jersey and parts of New York, Pennsylvania, and Maryland. He figured he can't travel that far considering everything."

"It's amazing how one man was able to get that many followers."

"Power."

They paused.

"Should we go look in that town back there?" the man holding the flashlight shined the light in the other's eyes.

"Worth a shot right?"

Sean and Paige couldn't out run these men. Lauren would not see these men coming. My eyes scanned the area. I clenched my fists.

"Hey morons," I shouted as I jumped out in plain view. "Is this the ass you're looking for?"

The light was shined on me and I bolted further into the darkness. No matter what happened to me I needed to make sure nothing happened to Lauren and the group. I was not going to let the group suffer for the mistakes I made in the past.

2
Aaron

My lungs were burning by the time that I lost the two idiots. Manson was in jail, why couldn't he have gotten real enemies there? Or at least not go for 'an eye for a whole head' exchange. I didn't see any beams examining the area so I sat on a tree stump and leaned over my knees to catch my breath. I needed water that was way too much running and moving for me to have done without drinking. Lifting my head I saw the faint puff in front of me.

Normally winter coming wouldn't phase me any, just meant occasionally throwing on a sweatshirt, but I was literally in the woods with nothing. Things were very serious right now. My eyes searched the area for a river or stream nearby. A person could last longer on no food than without water. I stood up and started to wander about looking for some water. A couple of squirrels scurried past me and up a tree. Watching those little furry animals, I wondered if they would taste like chicken. Wasn't that always the story, 'it takes like chicken?' No, I'll wait a little longer before thinking about eating a furry rat.

My foot caught on something, and I fell onto my back. Unable to grab onto anything I slid down the hill. My shirt got twisted together causing leaves, sticks, and a couple of rocks to scrape across my back. My bottom smacked against a rock stopping me short. Pain shot through me, and water started seeping through my jeans. Heat and throbbing radiated through my body as I tried to push myself up. I cursed at the rock that I ran into and pulled my feet out of the stream. If I had stayed with Lauren on the bed, I wouldn't have ended wet and in pain. I would be in the apartment with Sean and Paige trying to give them something to do before we killed them from cabin fever. Or I would be with Lauren who would probably be asleep against me for warmth. I closed my eyes for a moment to see those blue ones.

God damn it!

I kicked the water and got up. I had to stop thinking like that. That's why I left. I wasn't able to separate myself from the current situation of developing feelings for Lauren. She's suffering as it was without me in her life. I had a man out to kill me and she was still wounded from losing her family.

Scooping some of the water in my hands I tried to keep to the top of the water where there was less dirt. Better than nothing. I brought my cupped hands to my lips and sipped. Well, here's to running away. Again...

3

Aaron

The clouds were dark, but I was traveling a little in search of something to eat. My stomach was a little shaky probably from the water, but I figured I should eat none the less. Stepping out of the woods I came across a couple of homes. Their doors were thrown open in addition to their garage doors. There weren't any cars in them, the families probably grabbed what they could and escaped. I didn't blame them. If I had a family I'd pack up for safer grounds considering I could see the top of an asteroid on the other side of the houses. Rushing into the garage I listened to the inside, waiting to hear noises that someone else might have taken refuge in this abandoned home.

Silence.

Still I tiptoed into the house, but heard nothing. I went straight into the kitchen. The fridge didn't feel cool, they lost electricity. I started to shift through the cabinets. They had sporadic things in them, making it harder for me to find something that did not have mold or that had spoiled. Finally, I found some crackers and peanut butter. I took the packages with a knife and sat on the couch. I started to spread the peanut butter on the crackers, it felt like the food of the Gods. God, I hope that Lauren and the group had food. The cracker suddenly felt like cement in my throat. I had food and I wasn't even sure if the group did. I put the food down next to me feeling sick, I was spineless. My parents did not raise me to run away from my problems, but that seems to be all I was good at.

I stood up and went to the back door. Placing my fists on the glass I stared out into the backyard. The glass felt cool and it was then I realized how much warmer it was inside. The yard was pretty deep out and I kept my eyes out scanning the area as I zoned out.

I could see Sean tossing a baseball up in the air and catching it with a mitt. Paige chasing after Sean wanting to play too. Mandy was running alongside Paige to make sure that Sean played fair. Jill and Cole were in chairs in the sun, just as Jill gave Cole a shove so that his feet went over his head. I smiled just as Lauren who was laughing headed towards me. She reached out one of her hands towards me.

I shook my head and the sight of me vanished. God, I wasn't expecting to miss them this much. I glanced around the yard and noticed little raindrops. Ash mixed through the air as the rain came down harder creating almost a thick cloud closing around the house. Quickly I ran to the front door and closed it, and went around seeing if any of the windows were open. I slammed a couple of the windows before walking downstairs to where I left the food. Even the weather did not want me to go find Lauren right now. I was locked in this house for God only knows how long, alone with my thoughts. What could possibly go wrong?

That night I decided I finally needed to get some solid, real, sleep. The rain had subsided, but everything was still covered in a thick fog of ash. I was stuck inside the house for a little longer. I crept upstairs, my hand skimmed the railing with each step. Darkness had overtaken the house. Yet, a smirk grew on my face. The last time I tiptoed up some stairs in the dark I was greeted by Lauren who had wrapped her arms around my neck, pressing our bodies together as she wore nothing, but a nightshirt.

Shaking my head I found myself in one of the bedrooms and curled under the covers of the bed. Even though the windows and doors were closed the air was chilly around me. I just had to hope that Lauren was warmer than I was. My gut told me otherwise. Glancing to my other side I thought back to when I shared a bed with three other bodies plus two stuffed animals. I stared back at the ceiling and ran my fingers through my hair. What was wrong with me? Lauren was everywhere. I got away from her for this reason.

I took in a deep breath and let it out slowly. Lauren is just a girl. Lauren is just a girl. Lauren. Is. Just. A. Girl. Then why the hell could I not get her out of my head? I've been with girls before so Lauren shouldn't be any different. I tried to focus on the black of the inside of my eyelids. Between the frustration and temperature, I pulled the sheets over my head. Under the tent of blankets, I tried to calm my mind until I finally fell asleep.

4
Aaron

A week later and I was still at the house for a couple of reasons. First, I wanted to leave after the ash had dissipated. Second, I didn't know where else to go. There was not much food there, so I knew I had to be on the move at some point. Especially since there had been movement in the bushes. My hope was that there was some deer or bunnies moving around, but I was pretty sure since I thought I saw some flickering of lights. I was avoiding walking by the windows or the glass back door because every nerve of mine was on edge. Something was up.

Pacing around the master bedroom where I had been sleeping, I tried to think of a way out. Leaving when it was dark would be the best idea. Keeping flesh against the wall I glanced out the window. If I got a little bit of a running start I might be able to jump and grab onto one of the tree branches on that oak. I must be losing it. A running leap into a tree? My luck I'd miss the branch and break my neck. Well, that would be one way to get Manson off my back.

Looking out again the sky was full of oranges, pinks, and purples spreading across the sky. Whatever I was going to do, I was going to have to do it soon. I grabbed the jacket that I had found in the house, it was a little big on me, but I figured it was better than nothing. Walking into the bathroom I turned on the faucet and the water sprayed out in spurts. I grabbed a clean razor and wetted it with the water. I quickly shaved my face of peach fuzz before grabbing some scissors to trim my hair. Who knew when I'd get the chance again? I cut my hair to almost the scalp and put on a hat hoping to keep my head warm.

It probably was dumb to cut all my hair before I left, but not being able to wash my hair was getting to me. I couldn't imagine what Lauren felt about her own hair, it was much longer than mine. I thought back to when we first arrived at the house in Pennsylvania, and she showered. Her hair seemed like it would be soft to touch.

I shook my head and went to the window again. The bushes were rustling around the house. I cursed under my breath. They found me. I zipped the coat up and opened the window slowly. There were a couple of heads popping up around the trees and they were moving left to right. I crouched low to the frame and ducked my head. Once I had one foot over, I let the other half of my body follow suit. Keeping low to the roof though I crawled over to the tree. I stopped when I got close to the tree and watched a man go to the front door.

Taking my chance, I leaped to the tree with a thud. I bit my tongue to hold back the yell from the new bruises. Working quickly, I climbed down and ran down the street with shouts behind me. My feet hit the pavement and I tried to think of where I should go. A bullet whizzed by me and hit the car that I was near. Cursing I turned towards the woods, I tried to pick up my pace, yet not trip over any rocks. Dashing out of the woods when I heard leaves crushing behind me, I bolted for a nearby car and climbed into the back of the car. Once I was in the back I laid down and pulled a lone sweatshirt over my feet. Taking off my coat quickly and I draped it over my upper half. Closing my eyes, I tried to tune out my own racing heart to listen for footsteps. Slow breath in the nose. Hold. Hold. Release.

"Where the hell did, he go?" a voice in the distance yelled.

"People don't vanish, go look for him."

I tried to make my breathing even to limit the movement. I would be trapped with no place to escape to if they found me. The air was trapped in my throat though when I heard the footsteps near the car. I needed to live. I needed to be able to see the group again. I know I complained about them in the beginning, but I needed to live for them.

The sky was completely dark by the time I didn't hear any whispers or steps. Slowly sitting up I stayed on the floor to peek through the bottom of the windows. It seemed to be clear. I put my coat back on fell asleep in the backseat.

5
Aaron

The days were getting colder, and the days became a blur. It had snowed and I was thankful for the coat that I had stolen. I yanked on my cap to further cover my ears. When I was little, I loved the snow, I used to pretend that I was like Neil Armstrong with my boots leaving prints in the snow. My mom hated the cold, but she would bundle the two of us up on snow days to go outside. She would have snowball fights with me, always letting me win. We would stay outside until our noses and cheeks were pink then we'd go inside to get into our pajamas with a mug of hot chocolate for each of us. I watched the smoke form with the last breath I took. I was never going to see my mom ever again. The flash of her being disappointed

343

in the last time we spoke came before me.

I shook my head. I had to focus on the snow days, not my teen years with her. Staring at the clouds they were dark still from the snowstorm the night before.

"I hope you can see me up there. I'm trying to do better for you and dad."

My heart fell to my stomach. I needed to get back to Lauren. I could hear my mom's voice telling me that I shouldn't run away from my troubles. Though I'm pretty sure Lauren is exactly the type of girl my mom would've tried to set me up with. She didn't care for the ones that I brought home or the few that I did bring home. I chuckled, God, mom would try to marry Lauren and me together if she was still around. She wanted lots of grandchildren, well in the future.

My mom would make cookies with me sometimes after school, I think we ate more of the dough than the actual cookies. As much as my dad and I had a special relationship where he took me to get my tattoo, my mom was the one that I could talk to. She and I built a fort the first week that I moved in with them.

I shoved my hands into my pockets as I thought back to how nervous I was. I had spent the time that I could remember in a couple of foster homes before I was told I was getting adopted. I didn't trust my new parents. I had been shuffled around a few times that I didn't actually believe that they would keep me. I would barely talk to them, I picked at my food. I came down one morning to see a blanket fort in the living room with a plate of cinnamon buns inside.

I had tiptoed over to the blanket. They left me alone that day while I sat in the fort, and I fell asleep in it. The next morning, I woke up and saw my mom coming down the stairs. She had her hair tied back so that when she bent down to look at me, I could look into her eyes. She had the warmest smile that I had ever seen.

"I used to build forts like this for my cousin's when we were growing up. Do I still have the skills?"

I remember laughing and she asked to join me in the fort. When I nodded, she sat down next to me and talked about her family growing up. Eventually, I got hungry, and we ate breakfast. She got me. She always did. My mom got that I needed to do things on my time. She was the greatest mom.

"Mom, I know I never said it enough, but I love you. I promise I will make you proud. I didn't do much of that before you-" I paused unable to say out loud that she was gone. "I know I have to go back, even when you're gone, you're still steering me in the right direction."

I turned on my heel towards a certain girl.

6

Aaron

I thought I was going in the right direction. I was able to retrace my steps back to the abandoned house so that I could put myself in the right direction of the apartments. God, I hope that Lauren and the group did not move. She didn't move last time I left them, but how many chances would I be given? When you cared for someone, how many chances were they entitled to? My poor parents, I'm sure they gave me more chances than they should've, but Lauren wasn't my mom. I didn't love her, but I could not get her out of my head.

Oh, crud.

I had feelings for her. I kicked the ground before me. I was hoping that physically I was attractive to her because she was there. The upside-down stomach feeling when I looked into those eyes. The need to kiss her. Lauren took over my mind despite the months away from her. It all made sense now.

I screamed out and clenched my arm. I'd been shot. I pulled my hand to see it covered in red, there was a hole in my coat. Glancing over my shoulder I saw a man with a gun pointed at me. I had been too much in my own thoughts to keep my eyes open to my surroundings. I tried running away, jumping over a log as the woods started to spin.

"He went that way."

I cursed. I couldn't hide in the trees because there weren't any leaves left. There were footsteps behind me, they were heavy. I tripped over a rock and tumbled down the slight hill. Still holding my arm, I crawled on the ground until I reached a river. The men were right behind me. I inched closer to the water, I only had seconds. I took a deep breath and dunked myself under the water.

Needles stabbed me. Thousands upon thousands of needles felt like they were stabbing every inch of my body. Just when I wanted to burst through the water and yell out I saw figures moving on the hill, they looked in my direction but kept moving. When I thought my lungs would burst into flames the men were gone. Leaping out of the water my teeth chattered as my body shook uncontrollably. Looking around me I searched for wood and a couple of stones. I had a small pile of sticks, but my hands were shaking so much that I had trouble creating a fire. Just when I was about to give up a lone spark came to life, creating a fire.

I took off my coat and threw it on the floor. It was soaking wet and only causing me to shudder more. I slid my hat off my head and wrung it out. I went to rip the winter hat, but my hands kept trembling. I got frustrated that I brought the material to my teeth and did a hard yank until I heard a tear. I smiled as I wrapped the material around my wound and tied it tightly. The bullet only grazed me.

I threw some stones around the fire in a circle before I finally gave in to the need to rest. I leaned my head against my knees. I needed to get to Lauren and Sean. I could do this. I had never been so cold before in my entire life. I had to block it all out, I was close.

That night I was hardly able to get any sleep. I could not get warm, and I had to keep feeding the fire. I would have sold my left foot for a dry blanket. When the sun started to rise, I got up and stomped out the fire. Crossing my arms, I trudged on with my eyes barely able to stay open. Chills ran down my spine, but I kept putting one foot in front of the other. They had to still be there.

The sound of many voices reached my ears. I shook my head and glanced around searching for the source. The voices grew louder, and I felt déjà vu overcome me. I pushed aside the drowsiness and ran. Between the trees, I came across a road and buildings. People were yelling out. My knees almost gave out. My breath came out heavy with puffs of smoke.

My muscles I thought were ready to cave in, but I ran. Little Paige and Sean were in those buildings I knew it. Lauren, my Lauren was in there, I could feel it in my bones. There were fewer people outside on this winter day. Once I busted through the doors of the apartment, I saw people throwing things at each other, a person went to go throw a punch at another person. I leaped over a body with my heart pounding against my chest. With each step that I climbed the pain I was in seemed to dim and my smile grew until I was standing in front of a door. I raised my hand to knock to be allowed to be welcomed back into my life, my family.

Acknowledgements

Writing is something that I have always loved to do, but it is a journey that is a full of interesting turns. The people that have helped me along the way are not only people that I have known for years, but also new friends. End of the Line was my first book to be published, but for a point of time I had to unpublished the work. So the people who helped to get to the second edition were wonderful.

Taylor and I have known each other since sixth grade, started out in band then reconnected with each other in eighth grade when we had homeroom together. Taylor edited the first edition for me back in our senior year of High School. Despite all the computer trouble she had during that time she was able to edit the story. Taylor also had created the first edition's cover one night when we were hanging out.

Samantha was the first blogger to really

take me on. She not only reviewed the book, but also offered to help with the second edition. Also listened to when I started up drafting a second book.

My friend Amy Carrino and I have known each other for years. We were in band together in high school. Leave it to a couple of clarinets to stay connected over the years. While Amy edited the story, she helped make sure things were phrased correctly. We highly entertained ourselves with the comments she had for me as she went along. Amy did the cover for this edition. She had many pictures from her camping trips making it a hard decision.

Then there is Amy Eye. I first met her through Goodreads and her radio show. She is an awesome person who was unbelievably patient while editing End of the Line. She gave great tips and helped with loopholes that I hadn't thought of. If given the chance I would work with Amy again because it was a great experience.

Another great author I talk to is, Shawn Maravel. She has given me tips on writing not only for marketing, but also for grammar. Shawn is extremely sweet, and I am so thankful that I have met her for us to become friends. I am lucky enough to have countless family members who have all listened to and supported my writing. Not only do they read what they can, but they do what they can to help spread the word.

I love meeting people as I go along in life. Part of publishing is finding new people and helping each other out during the process. You are never done learning in life. I am thankful to anyone who can lend a hand and I try to return the favor to others.

About the author

In a fantastical land where the weather is always changing, not too far from the beach and the moon is high in a freckling sky Ottilie lives. This land is call New Jersey where she has lived her whole life and she mostly grew up in Wall Township. Ottilie is currently studying History Education at The College of New Jersey. Writing helps as a procrastination tool and a savior to her sanity. Ottilie has major support from her caring, supportive family along with her loveable, insane friends. She has two books out End of the Line and Family Ties!

You can find her on Facebook, Twitter, and her blog:
http://ottilieweber.blogspot.com

Other books by Ottilie Weber
End of the Lines series
End of the Line
Going Rogue
Off the Beaten Path

Family Ties Series
Family Ties
Invisible Bonds

Project US

A Storm on the Horizon

Beaker to Life

Mistakes Series
Shadows from the Past
Whispers from the Past
Footsteps in the Alley
A Howl for a Resistance
Moonlit Eyes

Beneath the Scars Series
Beneath the Scars
Call for Help
Define a Hero

Novellas
Best Friends
Treble with Music